MURDER IN THE MIDST
EIGHT DIFFERENT WOMEN. ONE THING IN COMMON: SERIOUS CRIME.

SANDI WALLACE

CONTENTS

Also by Sandi Wallace	vii
Fire on the Hill	1
Sweet Baby Dies	21
Abandon	41
Cheese, Wine and the Perfect Crime	61
The Witness	67
Ball and Chain	89
Gun Oil, Bacon and Bleach	109
Duplicity	131
Preview of Tell Me Why	151
Dear Reader	163
More of Sandi's Short Crime Stories	165
Acknowledgments	167
About the Author	169

Copyright (C) 2020 Sandi Wallace

Layout design and Copyright (C) 2020 by Next Chapter

Published 2020 by Gumshoe – A Next Chapter Imprint

Edited by Lorna Read

Cover art by Cover Mint

This book is a work of fiction. Names, characters, places, and incidents are the product of the author's imagination or are used fictitiously. Any resemblance to actual events, locales, or persons, living or dead, is purely coincidental.

All rights reserved. No part of this book may be reproduced or transmitted in any form or by any means, electronic or mechanical, including photocopying, recording, or by any information storage and retrieval system, without the author's permission.

PRAISE FOR SANDI WALLACE'S BOOKS

'A beautifully written police procedural, where the characters are every bit as important as the plot. Brilliantly captures the impact of small-town tragedy, as investigators struggle to cope even as they work towards solving an horrendous crime.'

— CHRIS HAMMER, WINNER OF THE UK CWA NEW BLOOD DAGGER AWARD FOR *SCRUBLANDS*

'Aussie Noir at its best. Once again Wallace has tapped into the rural crime genre with an iconic sense of place beneath a black cloud of menace and intrigue. Her Georgie Harvey and John Franklin series just gets better and better.'

— B. MICHAEL RADBURN, AUTHOR OF THE *TAYLOR BRIDGES* SERIES

'Sandi Wallace's best yet! Engaging, fast-paced, and full of suspense.'

— KAREN M. DAVIS, FORMER NSW POLICE DETECTIVE AND AUTHOR OF THE *LEXIE ROGERS* SERIES

'A gripping twist on the bushfire threat all Australians live with.'

— JAYE FORD, AWARD-WINNING AUTHOR OF *DARKEST PLACE*

'Suspenseful, exciting, atmospheric rural crime; a riveting debut.'

— MICHAELA LOBB, SISTERS IN CRIME AUSTRALIA

'Worthy debut.'

— *HERALD SUN*

'The police aspect of this novel has depth and believability…this debut is a cracker.'

— J.M. PEACE, SERVING QLD POLICE OFFICER AND AUTHOR OF AWARD-WINNING *A TIME TO RUN*

'Sharply crafted and authentic… These are stories that linger, long after they are read.'

— ISOBEL BLACKTHORN, REVIEWER, EDUCATOR, NOVELIST, POET

'Sandi Wallace packs as much punch into her short crime stories as she does into her novels.'

— ELAINE RAPHAEL, GOODREADS READER

ALSO BY SANDI WALLACE

Georgie Harvey & John Franklin novels

Tell Me Why
Dead Again
Into the Fog
Black Cloud

Short story collections

On the Job
Murder in the Midst

Award-winning short stories

'Sweet Baby Dies' *(Scarlet Stiletto: The Eleventh Cut – 2019)*
'Fire on the Hill' (*Scarlet Stiletto: The Tenth Cut – 2018*)
'Busted' (*Scarlet Stiletto: The Eighth Cut – 2016*)
'Ball and Chain' (*Scarlet Stiletto: The Sixth Cut – 2014*)
'Silk Versus Sierra' (*Scarlet Stiletto: The Fifth Cut – 2013*)

Non-fiction

Writing the Dream (contributing author)

To Judy, Raylea, Sharon and Marianne.

FIRE ON THE HILL

Winner Scarlet Stiletto Awards 2018
Best Romantic Suspense Story

First published in *Scarlet Stiletto: The Tenth Cut – 2018*

FIRE ON THE HILL

Charlie homed in on thrashing in the scrub. Someone on the run? She gestured to Gavin, did a zip motion over her mouth and indicated to fan out around their parked truck.

The sounds grew louder, closer, overlaid by groans that made the hairs on her forearm prickle. Her fingers closed on her holstered weapon. She tamped down the adrenaline buzz and controlled her breathing, lips barely parted and teeth filtering ash particles and hot air pungent with burnt eucalyptus oil. It was wrong to hope their offender was heading straight for them and carrying injuries – then again, no it wasn't.

Eyes skimming the bush shrouded in a bluey-orange haze, she crept forward. A koala emerged, then froze, apparently stunned by the two humans.

Charlie gave a surprised snort. Her chuckle became a cough and she reached for the water bottle slung over her shoulder. She took a swig, winced, sluiced and spat, while the animal watched her.

'Five minutes out of the esky and it's already half-stewed,' she told Gavin. But still parched, she shook her head and gulped some more of the tepid water.

As she wiped her mouth, the koala lifted its butt and bound to her feet, moving like a clumsy bunny. Stretching up on its hind legs, it reached towards Charlie's bottle with its front paws.

She crouched down. 'You want some, buddy?'

The koala pulled on her bottle with one paw and the other clasped onto her knee. Charlie dribbled water over its mouth and black nose. After it slurped up a few mouthfuls, she cupped her hand and held it near the ground, crooning until the animal drank from her palm. Each time she went to rise, the koala's curved claws bit tighter and it kept lapping until she'd emptied her bottle and Gavin's. Its thirst sated, the koala lumbered away.

'New nickname for you – Koala Whisperer.'

Get known as soft and she'd lose her standing in Howie. Charlie shook her head. 'Not.'

The corners of Gavin's grey-green eyes crinkled, then he turned serious. 'What're you thinking?'

She verbalised what had been on her mind since the fire siren yowled a few hours ago. 'Two separate seats of ignition about 400 metres apart. The male that called it in—first to the CFA, then to us direct, not via triple zero—was very specific with the details yet unwilling to give his name. He's our arsonist.'

He nodded.

'It could be an accomplice, but arsonists usually work alone unless they're profit-motivated or hiding other crimes – which doesn't seem to apply here.'

Gavin opened his mouth but was cut off by the peal of Charlie's phone: the name of the Howie fire captain on the screen.

'Neil?'

'Safe, Charlie.'

She let out a relieved sigh. If Neil's crew hadn't been so quick to contain the fire at Shanks Bend it might've burnt for days or longer, destroying thousands of hectares of forest, jeopardising the abutting properties…and perhaps the town.

It made Charlie suspect their man rang immediately after lighting the fire. Some semblance of conscience, or attention-seeking?

'We'll finish up here. Come by the shed – say, an hour?'

She promised they'd be there.

'Don't like it, Charlie.' Neil's face creased into furrows caked with soot. 'Not a bit.'

'You think they're escalating?' Charlie ran a hand up her neck, toying with copper-brown tendrils damp with perspiration.

Neil answered with a sigh as something dropped heavily behind him. She glanced over his shoulder, taking in a bundle of blackened yellow on the driveway. Then she scanned over booted feet and up dirty over-trousers to land on a naked, tanned torso.

She drew her eyes away and fixed again on the fire captain. 'Yeah, me too. The gap's shortened between the fires and they're getting –'

'Closer to town,' he finished.

Charlie grimaced. She had loved this little back-of-beyond place all her life, though merely as a frequent visitor before landing her first post here. Now she loved heading the cop shop that was only slightly less primitive than the fire brigade's oversized tin shed. If she couldn't catch the cocky arsonist, everything that mattered was at risk.

Absently, her gaze floated to the set of broad shoulders and biceps snaked with tattoos belonging to the guy behind Neil. He rubbed his fingers through his cropped, black hair and chatted easily. Charlie knew the crew well, but she wasn't familiar with this volunteer.

She scuffed her boots in the dust, mind back on the job. 'We're going to need Roger.'

Neil nodded.

'Let's hope he's not tied up.'

She'd take any available fire investigator, but Roger was exceptional, and he had been born and bred in Howie. He knew the trouble ahead for their little town if the arsonist kept at it…and these people never stopped voluntarily.

The captain said, 'Makes you wish they never built Howie on top of the hill, doesn't it?'

'And it wasn't surrounded by bush.'

An ill-timed rumbling chuckle made her peer at the new firie. She watched his trousers join the rest of his turnout gear. Now he wore nothing but board shorts. And he belonged on a calendar for Country Fire Authority fundraising.

Charlie's portable radio squawked, and the new guy looked across, smiling at whatever Neil's deputy, Pauline, had said. His head-tilt gave away that he'd caught Charlie's stare. She went for her radio as Gavin rushed to her side. Her embarrassment heightened. Gavin never missed a thing – a good and bad attribute in her right-hand man.

He was still hovering when she ended the radio call and focused again on Neil.

She said, 'We'll go back to Shanks in case our man's returned.'

Both men nodded, then Neil stepped sideways to let the board-shorts guy join their huddle. He waved between them. 'You haven't met Dylan properly.'

Over introductions, Charlie shook the tall firie's hand, dodging his deep blue eyes but tuning into his lilting accent.

'Irish?'

'No, but close.' His voice glided high and low. 'Welsh.'

'He's only been in town a few weeks.'

Gavin's chin gave a jerk. Charlie didn't like the coincidence either, but the captain was a good judge of character. If he didn't find the overlap of their arson attacks and Dylan Owen's arrival suss, she probably shouldn't, either.

'Works at O'Shaunessy's,' Neil continued.

As Howie's largest employer, if the vineyard closed, they'd all be in trouble. It propped up most of the other businesses—even the cop shop could end up abandoned with Charlie, Gavin and the others lucky to be redeployed to Wangaratta or Mansfield—though about a third of those working at O'Shaunessy's were transients, mostly seasonal workers from overseas.

'On his way up the ranks there.'

Dylan agreed, but it was hard to take him seriously wearing just board shorts. Charlie pegged him as a charmer, a backpacker and likely to be gone by Christmas.

He said, 'A week in the forties and only the tenth day of summer – are you worried, Captain?'

Neil's forehead took on more lines. 'It's not looking good.'

A line of sweat ran down Charlie's back. Four fires in the nearby bush this December, none natural – her first fire season as sergeant-in-charge at Howie and third working in the town was already the worst she'd ever tackled.

Dylan spoke again. 'We're all going for drinks later. Charlie…be seeing you?'

She felt like a pinned bug as three sets of eyes turned to her.

Gavin touched her shoulder and answered, 'We'll be there.'

'Maybe.' She shrugged off his hand. 'Time to go, Senior Constable.'

Dylan's low chuckle followed them as she and Gavin moved to the marked truck. She regretted pulling rank but couldn't undo it. If black-haired Dylan could grace a Hot

Firies calendar, then Gavin could be his blond cop counterpart, and he was as off-limits as the charismatic potential fire bug.

They returned to Shanks Bend in a strained silence broken only by the squeaks of the truck's suspension, thuds as sticks and rocks hit its underbelly and spatters from the police radio.

Gavin's hurt was palpable right through the rest of their shift and Charlie eventually mollified him for the sake of workplace peace.

'See you at the pub later, Gav-Man?'

She used the station nickname to make it clear they were going as mates, but suspected he didn't get it when he grinned and named a time.

Charlie craved a long shower, but the town's water reserves were critical. She made do with a ninety-second soap and scrub under the water-saver outlet. Her hair was still infused with eau de bushfire when she strolled into The Junction, Howie's only pub. Maybe all she had to do was work her way through the place, sniff for burnt bush aroma and wait for the arsonist to give themselves away?

She laughed at the dumb idea and greeted her friend Sammi over the counter.

'Gavin's got your usual, Char.' The publican grinned, her cheeks dimpling and a gleam in her nut-brown eyes. 'Where can I find a fella like that?'

Her wave fanned over the room, as a guy in a blue singlet and shabby cargo shorts butted in with, 'Where's the sheila's trough for me missus?'

'You mean the ladies toilet –?' Sammi's eyebrows lifted.

Her friend's point well made about the quality of some men in Howie, Charlie scanned over the faces and spotted

Gavin at a table with two empty wine glasses and a bottle of red in front of him. She made her way over and was bemused when the new firie promptly joined them.

'G'day, Dylan.'

Gavin smiled as he shook hands with the Welshman. His expression turned guarded as Charlie did likewise. But she was distracted by the scents of the two men: strong citrus aftershave emanating from Gavin's red-blotched neck and a musky rum from Dylan…overladen with smoke. Not surprising – they'd all spent most of the day at Shanks Bend.

Charlie missed an exchange between the two guys and wasn't sure how it came about, but somehow the three of them ended up seated around the table, sipping wine and planning their counter meals.

She let the guys do most of the talking, her mind obsessing over the arsonist. The attacks were coming faster together and increasingly close to town. Roger would be able to determine more from the fire scenes than she and Neil, identifying accelerants and materials used and behavioural patterns that might help Charlie and her team pinpoint and arrest the offender. But he was working a job in Rutherglen and couldn't get to them until lunchtime tomorrow.

That might be too late.

She felt the pull of Dylan's blue eyes as he said, 'You're worried?'

'Yes.'

Charlie was torn. It was unethical to share the police investigation with a civilian and virtual stranger, but something about him tempted her. With a sense that they had to act quickly or face another—worse—fire attack, she wondered if a fresh perspective might help.

Given the coincidence of this guy's arrival in town and the spree starting, she'd be selective though.

'We don't have any witnesses or evidence that points to

anyone – yet. But we've got a fire investigator coming tomorrow.'

Dylan nodded, and Charlie went on. 'Gavin and I have knocked on doors of known arsonists – anyone, in fact, that we suspect might light fires.'

Her offsider gave her a strange look, adding, 'We put them on notice they're being watched.'

The firie's eyes flared, again drawing her in. His accent thickened with a roll of the r sounds as he said, 'But if they haven't come to your attention so far…'

Charlie shrugged, cutting eye contact. She noticed that Gavin's gaze was fixed on Dylan, a small frown pulling between his brows.

Overprotective, jealous, or sensing something off about the newcomer?

She huffed under her breath. They said women could be complicated and challenging to work with, while men were easier because they called a spade a spade. Whoever *they* were hadn't worked with Gavin.

She needed a timeout and excused herself.

Charlie wove through the throng and went onto the front verandah of the low-slung hotel. In the shade of the wide, bullnosed roof the air was still oppressive – as hot, unmoving and dry as the rest of the day had been. Another impossible sleeping night. But that was a given with an arsonist at large.

They had so little to go on. Pregnant and mostly desk-bound at the station, Gemma had taken each of the calls. The constable assessed they were made by a male somewhere between thirty and fifty, his speech muffled and accent hard to pick. He'd been hurried and hung up in under thirty seconds. Same number: a disposable mobile.

Feeling desperate, Charlie re-entered the pub and tried the number. She listened to it ring on her handset. Strained to hear an echo somewhere in the room. Considered faces for shock or guilt. Expected the call to ring out and nothing to come from the experiment. Very surprised when the phone was answered.

Sammi's tinkling laughter came through the open line and into Charlie's uncovered ear.

The arsonist was here.

She scoped the room. Gavin and Dylan stood with their backs to her. Sammi and her staff virtually danced behind the bar, serving and entertaining regulars. Other patrons filled tables and stools, played pool, leaned on pillars or walls.

The majority were men and too many held mobile phones.

Charlie skimmed again. Both Gavin and Dylan had disappeared. A couple of guys had phones pressed to their ears. She spotted a mobile on a ledge near the back door with nobody near it and her stomach sank. She didn't need to redial the last number she'd called to realise she'd stuffed up the one lead they'd had.

She bolted anyway, swiped up the phone and pushed through the back door. The only people in sight were a couple writhing together, limbs, long hair and torsos meshed.

She yelled, 'Did anyone just come out?'

The women parted for long enough to say no.

Charlie ran through the car park, throwing glances in every direction including under the vehicles. She wouldn't give up until she'd checked the beer garden and right around the perimeter, questioning anyone in sight. But she knew the man was gone.

Two plates of food were growing cold and Charlie was scraping hers clean. If Dylan and Gavin didn't return soon, she'd give theirs to the Beattie sisters; they were gaunt and always dressed in clean but faded and thin clothing and would benefit from a free feed.

She placed her cutlery on her empty plate and startled when a voice said, 'You're not going yet?'

Dylan.

And at his shoulder, Gavin. Both chuckling. Gavin was holding an upended CFA helmet, wearing a goofy grin.

'Where have you been?' Too sharp, but she could've done with his help before.

'Meeting Daisy.'

The helmet was shoved into Charlie's hands and she saw a cream puppy nestled inside the liner, velvety belly upwards, rising and falling as it snored softly.

'My little girl.'

She glanced at Dylan. 'You've got a dog?' Seemed irresponsible for a transient worker.

He smiled. 'O'Shaunessy's are sponsoring my resident visa and extra studies in winemaking.' He indicated to their bottle of the local shiraz. 'They see me taking over from my boss when he retires.' His blue irises drew her in. 'I've been working in the region for nearly a year. I like Howie.'

His eyes twinkled. 'A lot now. I'm not passing through, Charlie.'

Lovely roll on the r in Charlie. A jolt in her lower tummy. Buzzing in her nerves when Dylan pressed in to stroke the sleeping puppy, making her conscious of the hard, black-inked muscles of his arm.

Puppies, tatts and arm muscles…and she had an arsonist to catch.

Annoyed with herself, she started to thrust the helmet at him when one of the old-timers hollered, 'Fire on the hill!'

He pointed.

Everyone swarmed for the front verandah, but they made way for Charlie, Gavin and Dylan. Neil appeared next to them.

For a few seconds, they stared at the ominous orange glow on the dusky horizon. Charlie got the shakes. She felt the weight lifted from her arms, distantly heard Sammi say, 'I'll take Daisy. You guys go.'

The cold numbness grew inside her when Neil confirmed her fear. 'That's Maureen's place isn't it, Charlie?'

She moaned. 'Nan.'

Someone took her hand, gave it a gentle squeeze. She recognised it was Dylan, his firie helmet tucked under his arm, blue eyes steely. The gesture fortified her. She closed her fingers around his, then released the hold. Took off at a jog for the marked four-wheel drive, Gavin at her heels.

Over the bedlam of the wailing fire siren, people shouting and rushing to vehicles or for the fire house, Charlie picked up Dylan's promise 'I'll meet you there.' Or maybe she'd imagined it. But again, she felt a surge inside. Galvanised, determined to protect her dear nan. Not so sure she could do the same for the century-old farm buildings.

Before jumping in the truck, she and Gavin pulled on their fire-retardant coveralls and boots. The rest of their emergency gear was inside, repacked after today's efforts at Shanks Bend. Between all this, Gavin called their other guys – off-duty or not, they were needed.

He said, 'I'll drive.'

'No.' Charlie shook her head. 'I know the area better.'

They might need to detour on- or off-road for trees down or spot fires. She ground her jaw, thinking sabotage wasn't impossible.

'Get Nan on my phone, Gavin.'

He took her mobile and scrolled. Rings came through the truck's Bluetooth, then the call connected.

'Nan?'

'Char? That you?'

'Are you okay?'

'I was having a read after tea and dozed off. The garage is on fire, Char.' She paused. *'And the old dairy.'*

Though she'd recently celebrated her seventy-eighth birthday, Nan was robust in all ways. But she sounded frightened, brittle, when she said, *'Who…what are…no –'*

The call ended.

Charlie's pulse boomed in her ears.

She and Gavin exchanged a stricken glance. There were no words to describe how she felt, and he knew her well enough to understand and anticipate her moves.

Charlie drove the truck as hard as the conditions allowed. Gavin braced against the body roll and tried to reach Nan a second time. No success.

Coming into Nan's road, the truck's headlights struggled against the thickening smoke. Charlie sat forward and strained to see through the windscreen, while Gavin maintained a steady commentary on the radio or his mobile. He was doing a good job.

The front gate sat ajar. Some CFA vehicles had beaten their arrival. As their truck cleared the crossover, the mounting sounds of sirens and snarling flames were outdone by a scared voice in Charlie's head begging for Nan to be unharmed.

Her best childhood memories all started with her hopping out of the family car to open the wide, pipe-frame and mesh gate. Her excitement mounting as they wound up the gravel driveway, past the orchard, the dam, the front paddocks with cows and alpacas.

The hedge of bushy gums dividing Nan's top paddocks was ablaze and a separate grassfire seared a path leading to the front of the house. Fortunately, Charlie had helped Nan rotate all the stock last week and the animals appeared to be safe. For now. The garage was a burnt-out shell; the dairy halfway gone. Flames licked the wall of Nan's lounge room.

Charlie parked, exited the truck and grabbed her gear. She registered Gavin doing likewise while he updated central communications. She saw a firie in full kit wave and run to her. She recognised Dylan's build and gait – he a stranger a few hours ago, inexplicably her lifeline now.

They jogged together, their voices muffled by masks.

'Any sign of my nan?'

'No. But we haven't been inside yet.'

They drew next to Neil, pausing for Charlie to say, 'We'll loop around to the back door – get Maureen out, if she's in there.'

He nodded, and Charlie and Dylan took off again in a lumbering run. She kept chewing over the potent message the arsonist had sent tonight. This was more than acceleration or coincidence. He'd pointed the attack at a person she loved who was alone and vulnerable. He'd intended to cause significant destruction. To kill?

This was personal for her and it made sense that it must be for him, too.

She considered her ex-boyfriends and ruled them out. It had to relate to the job. She ran through names and faces, recent incidents and conflict. Each fire attack occurred close to Howie, so the offender must be a local. And to do this to her nan—who everyone adored—he hated Charlie.

'Nan! It's Char! Where are you?'

She heard a window shatter in the direction of the lounge room and picked up speed.

She and Dylan circled away from the grassfire and chaos of people hastening to set up hoses and equipment. Running for the back door of the homestead, her mind kept ticking over. For the arsonist to target someone she loved, his hurt might well be relationship-based. The most acrimonious of marriage breakdowns, perhaps. Who had she contended with in a custody dispute? Slapped on an intervention order? Thrown in the cells to cool off? Been instrumental in getting sentenced?

They passed the laundry and she screamed, 'Nan, are you in there?'

Dylan reached the flywire door two seconds before Charlie. He pulled it open and seemed to be listening and assessing the dangers.

'I'm going in. With my nan in there –' Charlie pushed into the lean-to as he nodded behind his mask.

'Nan?' Her voice cracked as she was hit with a realisation – the arsonist was Ryan Healy.

Healy had seen red when he discovered his pregnant wife was sleeping with the local mechanic. He'd gone for a drive—plastered—crashed into and written off his neighbour's car. Charlie had suspended his licence and charged him with driving intoxicated and reckless driving. Next incident saw him plough a borrowed car through the front fence of his in-laws' house where his estranged wife was now living. Charlie had mopped up that one, too and she'd also been the one to apprehend him after he'd abducted his wife – or, as he put it, *Took her for a drive to talk things through*. And Charlie certainly wasn't flavour of the month when she'd subsequently served Healy with an IVO.

Each time, Healy had gone for car keys, not matches. Beyond dragging his ex into the car, he hadn't physically assaulted anyone. Charlie hadn't anticipated that he'd act out next by lighting a fire. So, when the fires started the month after Healy's world imploded, she hadn't connected the dots.

She'd stuffed up. And when he thought she'd spotted him at the pub, he'd seen red again and decided his last gasp was going to be dramatic and aimed straight at Charlie's heart.

'Nan?'

Dylan flanked her, calling, 'Maureen?'

An almost-empty beer glass and a novel sat abandoned next to Nan's favourite reading chair in the sunroom. This was where she must've fallen asleep, oblivious to the fires being lit around her. But Nan wasn't there, or in the adjacent laundry and loo.

Charlie surged for the panelled door separating the sunroom and kitchen. Dylan said something she couldn't hear, and she swung the door and stepped over the threshold. She cried out at a sharp whack to the top of her helmet, then her right shoulder.

Dylan's arms wrapped around her, his body shielding her as he lifted her to safety. Charlie scrambled free, ready to slam Healy to the floor and demand he tell her where her nan was.

There was nobody else in the kitchen.

Charlie stared at sticks of timber and rope scattered near the door. 'He booby-trapped it.'

Dylan's helmet moved in a nod.

'But judging by that, he probably only meant it to slow us down.'

'Yes. Though it would've hurt more without this.' He touched the brim of her helmet.

Charlie said, 'She's not here.'

'Stay together as we search.'

'No, yeah…what I mean is, I don't think Nan's in the house, but yes, we have to be sure.'

They searched the bathroom and bedrooms while Charlie summarised her theory on Healy. Only one room left.

The torrent of water pounding on the tin roof and duller thuds as it streamed against the weatherboard cladding gave her hope the firies could save Nan's home. But smoke wisped under the closed lounge room door. Her stomach dropped when a whoosh sound overrode the crackling – the fire had taken hold of something in there. If Nan was inside, she'd be overcome by smoke.

'Me this time.' Dylan forced eye contact through their protective shields. 'My job.'

She stepped aside to let him take the lead. He inched open the door, and heat and noise and smoke assaulted her every sense. But once they'd eased in, Charlie expelled a breath. It was better than she'd expected. The fire was contained to the curtains and a single lining-board wall. Water, ash, scorched timber and glass fragments littering the hardwood floorboards were mostly confined to one area.

Thorough check. No Nan.

From where they stood, Charlie looked down at the rear of the farmhouse and she had a 180-degree view of the property. She could see a growing mass of CFA appliances and uniformed firies working hard to control the blaze. She dragged in air, thankful to have the helmet and face gear off, and followed Dylan's side of his conversation with Neil.

'So, you're winning down there?' He listened to the fire captain and gave Charlie a nod. 'We'll keep searching for Maureen.'

He hung up. 'Unless the wind changes, they expect to be on top of it soon.' Pointing to a cluster of men and women in civvies clearing a firebreak on the boundary, he added, 'Your nan has good neighbours.'

'Yes, she does.' Charlie's voice was gravelly. It was all pointless if they couldn't save Nan.

She scanned back over the scene and spoke again. 'Don't make it obvious…but check the ridge behind me. What can you see?'

Dylan's eyes skimmed over the hill. She drew a breath when his jaw slackened.

'A parked vehicle. Someone inside…no, two people. How'd –?'

She grasped his elbow. 'Nan?'

'I can't tell.'

'Describe the –'

'Chrome grill. Duco is cream or beige.'

'An old Holden ute?'

He'd barely nodded before Charlie started walking.

'I think Healy's up there, with Nan, in her paddock basher. We'll skirt around and sneak up from behind.'

She wanted to sprint but couldn't risk scaring off Healy. Her breath hitched, fear for her nan making it hard to fill her lungs. Dylan's presence at her side helped. So did his arm slipping around her shoulders for a few seconds.

Charlie phoned Gavin as they rounded the ruins of the original cottage, out of view from the parked car. Gavin and their lanky constable Wes would set off immediately, but she couldn't wait for their backup. God knows what Healy might do to her nan.

She mouthed *Be quiet* to Dylan as they entered a thick patch of scrub. They picked their way through, careful not to snap the dry litter. Close enough to hear a male's voice—the defensive *poor me* tone Healy had used in their recent encounters—and Nan's occasional interjections.

Charlie crouched, Dylan copied, and they sidled up on the ute. The sight of a jerrycan lying outside the driver's door made her heart pound. The stench of petrol reaching her nostrils sickened her to the pit of her stomach.

The temperature was still in the mid-thirties, and the grass here was mid-calf height and crispy dry. If the ute's cabin or its occupants were doused in fuel, one spark would be deadly. Charlie drew her weapon but couldn't risk using it…or letting Healy turn over the ignition.

She gestured to Dylan and they raced to either side of the vehicle.

She yelled, 'Hands up, Healy! Don't do anything stupid!'

Healy twisted towards her voice. She flinched when his left hand arced up through the air, his thumb on the ignition button of a lighter and almost touching the spark wheel.

'Stay back or we all go boom!'

Dylan had opened the passenger door, but Nan was

inclined away from him. Her face was framed by Healy's upraised arm. Pale and grim, it then took a determined set. She sliced her hand down on the base of Healy's thumb. His grip on the lighter loosened and she flicked it away.

Nan glared at him. 'For goodness' sake, Ryan.'

Charlie watched, stunned – also afraid any movement would be catastrophic.

'You told me before you never meant any of this to happen. You never meant to start lighting fires, but you were hurting and wanted to let that out. You went driving and there was your lighter.'

Nan laid a hand over Healy's, which had dropped to clutch the steering wheel. 'You told me you were sorry.'

Charlie reached through the open window and slid the key from the ignition. She slowly released Healy's door and said, 'Ready to come out?'

He nodded and stumbled from the ute, lifting his hands above his head.

'Good man.' She frisked him, cuffed him and when his legs gave way, helped him sit on the ground, back against a tree.

After he'd recovered, she led him over to Dylan and Nan.

Dylan was introducing himself and he still held her nan's hand. He lowered his voice, sounding more Welsh than ever as he said, 'I hope to be seeing a lot of you, Maureen.'

His eyes, deep blue and glittering, swept to Charlie. 'And you –?'

She took in his rugged features, sooty turnout gear and his hopeful, yet unsure expression.

A few beats went by, then she said, 'Maybe – I do like Daisy.'

His face fell, and she chuckled, giving him a slow wink.

SWEET BABY DIES

Winner Scarlet Stiletto Awards 2019
Best Romantic Suspense Story

First published in *Scarlet Stiletto: The Eleventh Cut – 2019*

SWEET BABY DIES

He had her pressed against the wall, his pants around his ankles. One hand pinned her arms above her head and the other cupped her bare butt. The series of fast-action shots left no doubt about what he was doing, and that the pretty young thing he was doing it with wasn't his wife. It wasn't even the pretty young thing he'd done the dance with last week. He was a goner and once I put my report together for his wife, that'd be a wrap on this file.

I spent a minute daydreaming. With any luck, I'd land another case today – something exciting. I should've touched wood.

'Mickey!'

I went through to the boss's office and hooked my eyebrows when I spotted a young dude in one of the armchairs.

Kurt handed over a file.

'Priority job. And the newbie is going to tag along and see how it's done.' He pointed. 'Andre Marchese, meet Mickey Fox. She's my best investigator.' A pause, then he added, 'Surprising, really.'

'Because I'm a woman?'

He didn't mean it that way, and Kurt and I exchanged grins. The newbie's eyes darted to my wheelchair.

'Follow me.'

I hooked a finger in the air and led him to my small office. At my desk, I flipped through the file, jotted notes and plugged key info into the case app, while Andre propped and watched, a kind of awe in his eyes. Nothing I'd done so far warranted it, but I dug it.

'How did you get into this?'

'I wanted to join the police. Failed the physical.' I gestured at my body, mocking disbelief.

He spluttered.

'Anyway, I love it.' Serving back the same question, I added, 'Is this your dream job? Or a stepping stone?'

Andre lifted his hands. 'Dream job. Weird or what?'

'That'd be a case of the pot and kettle, wouldn't it?' I pushed back from the desk. 'Our first stop's a few blocks away. Let's walk.'

He flushed.

'You need to lighten up, Andre.' A smile softened my words and I could see he had more questions, but Kurt had ASAP'd this job, so they'd have to wait.

The automatic sliding doors sucked closed behind us as we exited HQ. We hit the footpath, heat pulsating off the concrete around us, and me doing a bad rendition of the *Wanted Dead or Alive* chorus, extra emphasis on the *steel horse* bit. The whirling of my wheels reminded me of a clock turning and that Andre was alongside for practical experience.

I quickened my pace and filled him in on the case.

'Our subject is a commercial litigation lawyer.' I named the firm; one of Melbourne's big six. 'Pretty much anyone working in the legal rat race takes lunch at 1.00pm. So,' I checked the time, 'we have seven minutes to position ourselves.'

He nodded, and we hurried on, making our way through the posh marble expanse of the high-rise foyer and by lift to the tenth floor, getting there with two minutes to spare.

Andre whispered, 'Now what?'

I flashed him an image on my phone and he caught on. Making idle chat, I watched to the left and he the right, scanning faces as employees spilled out via reception. We just had to hope Erica Vaucluse wasn't a paper-bag-luncher or out on one of those famous long, liquid, lawyer's lunches.

He mouthed *She's coming*.

I winked in acknowledgement, shifted my weight to twist the wheels of my chair, and gave them a strong shove with both hands, calling out a cheery, 'Erica!'

She smiled automatically, pausing long enough for me to roll forward, extract a large envelope and thrust it into her hands. 'Erica Vaucluse. You've been served.'

I'd expected more of a challenge from a litigation lawyer and felt slightly ripped off. Anticipating she'd make up for it with a feisty reaction, I backed away, adhering to Kurt's golden rule *Never take your eyes off the subject*.

But nothing happened. She didn't curse, cry or threaten me. Merely used a manicured, clear-polished nail to slit the envelope. If my eyes weren't pinned to her face as she tipped out the subpoena and scanned the first page, I would have missed the skin under its layer of golden beige foundation paling and her eyes glazing. Her bearing more than guarded. *Fearful?*

It gave me a jolt. A case was a case and it wasn't my place to get personally involved. But—and I'd never admit this aloud—I liked to think we were hired by the nice guys and worked on the right side of good, upholding the moral high ground and all that jazz.

There was no doubting it, though. Erica Vaucluse's

response to being served looked to me as genuine, albeit restrained, alarm. And as the four-inch heels on her pumps tapped away on the tiled floor as she retreated to the office, her body was held tense inside its classy black pantsuit.

After that, Andre and I had time to kill. I suggested one of my favourite cafés and we took a table on the shady side of Centre Place, on a footpath so narrow that the right wheel of my chair balanced precariously on the edge. I soaked in the eclectic mix of locals and tourists, grungy street art covering the walls and roller doors, and a busker who managed to sing, strum an acoustic guitar and use his socked foot to play a half-tambourine all at once. A breeze stirred the warm air, flapping my tunic singlet against my skin in a soothing rhythm.

But my thoughts reverted to Erica. Worrying about my subject's wellbeing came with a dose of guilt for breaking the PI code. At least we weren't done with the file yet, so I could legitimately keep tabs on her.

The clunk of a mug on the table drew my attention. Andre fixed his eyes on mine, making me think of the dark-roasted coffee we'd just consumed. His fingertips played over the neat stubble on his jawline.

I sensed his question before it came.

'How did you –?' he trailed off.

All that build-up and he can't do it.

I touched the arm of my chair. 'How did me and BJ get together, you mean?'

He nodded.

'Car accident when I was sixteen.'

His expression was a giveaway; I helped him work it out.

'Nine years ago.' I held out my hands. 'Dad was driving. I was in the passenger seat. Front-end, engine, dash, airbag, my legs…' At my compacting motion, he shuddered.

There was a pause, then he said tentatively, 'And your dad?'

I raised my hands, then let them drop.

'Physically, pretty good. Whiplash for about six months and a dodgy shoulder ever since. But mentally, well, he's never forgiven himself, even though he wasn't at fault and I've never blamed him.'

I shrugged, and we didn't talk for a while. Happy to be done with the disability questions, I added the time, date and place of service to Vaucluse's file on the case app. Andre bobbed his head lightly to the busker's tunes.

When I tucked away my phone and tablet, he was giving me another odd look.

'What's on your mind?'

'Isn't it hard to do the job in,' he hesitated, then came up with, 'BJ,' visibly pleased to think of something other than *a wheelchair*.

'Nah. It's a great disguise. People don't notice the woman in the wheelchair, just the chair.' He cringed and I laughed. 'It's a fact.'

For a moment, I dropped my guard and went serious.

'Foot pursuits are obviously a problem, but my Honda's modified, BJ's got most of the features of elite sports chairs, and public transport's manageable. Besides, most of our work calls for brains over leg power.'

He hung on my words, nodding repeatedly. I had to lighten things up again.

Flexing, then straightening my bare left arm, I flaunted the defined muscles from my shoulder to wrist. 'Now, without my upper body strength, I'd be stuffed as a PI.'

When I chuckled again, he joined in. Relieved, I gave my watch a tap. 'Time to prepare for round two: surveillance.'

Andre's response gave me a glimpse of what he'd been like at school: front-row keeno with his hand up to answer every question. He sprang out of his seat and paid the bill as I did a neat 180. We returned to HQ, while he fired off more things on his mind.

'Who's our client? Are we often hired for process service *and* surveillance? What are we hoping to see?'

Good questions from the newbie.

I answered in order.

'The subject's soon-to-be-ex hubby – did I mention that he used one of ours to deliver her divorce papers last week? Not often, but I've handled a few with both. Presumably we'll know when we see it – my educated guess is he's pushing her buttons every which way to make sure the settlement goes in his favour.'

'From love to hate,' he murmured.

Right then, a toddler screamed until its face was a howling tomato. Response enough.

'That's mine.' Andre pointed to an older model Suzuki Swift. 'We could use it rather than pick up yours?'

His tone unconfident, I jumped in. 'Makes sense.'

It was suitably nondescript for our needs. And it wasn't the worst car to get in or out of. But my headspace got crowded with logistics. With nine years' experience, I could fold and stash BJ in the boot in under a minute. The subsequent ungainly crab-walk to the cabin was something I preferred doing without an audience, but that'd never stopped me.

Andre mooted the option by steering me alongside the car. Closing in, I noted one ding and two scratches to the blue duco that I'd make certain not to add to.

Once he'd opened the passenger door, I calculated the best spots for me to grip. I locked BJ's brake, then looped my hands around a knee and thigh to raise my foot off the plate and lower each leg. Discreetly, my fingers dug through my trousers to lock my callipers. Then I readied my shoulders, hands and core for the process of hoisting myself to the edge of the seat and wiggling up to grab onto the car.

All sorted, until Andre threaded an arm around my waist and drew me out of BJ.

'I've got you.'

Sure, he thought he did, but the unexpected action caused me to teeter. *I don't need help* rose to the tip of my tongue, but I swallowed the retort. We were still joined in an awkward clinch, but I brought off a clumsy rotation and landed heavily on the seat. My face heated, and he looked equally mortified.

'Leave it to me next time.'

He nodded and swept away the chair. Hearing him struggle to get BJ into the boot, I shrunk deeper into the bucket seat.

He climbed behind the wheel. 'Um…' His blush sent me into chuckles.

I tried to explain. 'Anyone glancing through the windscreen right now would see two red-faced people looking uptight. They'd think we're an item and fighting over something dumb.'

He gave a burst of laughter. 'Never a dull moment with you, Mickey.'

I placed a hand to my chest and joked, 'I'll take that as a compliment, I think?'

'You should.'

Our gaze met, then broke as he fired the ignition. 'Where to?'

He followed my directions to the car park under the subject's office building. To the hum of the running engine, we watched the exit from the laneway.

'She drives a pearl-grey, five-door Audi SQ5 SUV.' I recited the rego.

'She tends to leave between 5.00 and 5.30pm – some exceptions, like when she's in trial. Her dictaphone gets a workout on her drive home to Park Orchards, and after tea with her two daughters she spends several more hours in her home office.'

'Pity she needs sleep, or she could work 24-7.' Andre pulled a face.

'She gets out a few evenings a week.' I matched his expression. 'Apparently that's as unexciting as the rest of her time, but maybe we'll get lucky. Her soon-to-be-ex must be counting on it.'

A few cars trickled out of the car park over the next thirty minutes, while a mass of support staff spewed from the main entrance and rushed for public transport. I wondered how Erica Vaucluse had wrangled family-friendly office hours and an equity partnership, figuring she must be damn good at her job.

'Let's give it another ten.'

I used five of those minutes to run backgrounds on the names I'd glimpsed on the subpoena: Orbolt Holdings and McLeod-Dixon Enterprises.

According to the web, OH was a property, fiscal and environmental entrepreneurship specialist—whatever that meant—while MDE was into research and technology. From there, it seemed opaque, if not fishy, and my mind wandered into what sort of deal they'd been involved in that'd gone sour, and how Vaucluse and Vaucluse tied in.

After another two minutes, I'd discovered our client was on the board of OH and he was a property lawyer for a different Collins Street firm.

I wasted the rest of the extra ten shooting blanks on his wife and wishing I'd seen the schedule attached to the Form 42C specifying what evidence she had to give and produce at the upcoming Supreme Court trial, and speculating about why that, potentially combined with the recent divorce papers, frightened her.

The little I'd uncovered so far pointed to big money and powerful players. To be where she was on the lawyer ladder, Erica Vaucluse evidently knew how to play with both. But in the time that it took for Andre to drop me and BJ outside my ground-floor apartment in Balaclava, I mulled over whether this was in a whole different league – if she was in physical danger.

While I changed and applied a lick of lipstick and mascara, my thoughts twisted. Maybe Andre had nailed it with *From love to hate*. Her hubby was prepared to pull out all the stops, including tying Erica into corporate litigation. If he hated with the same passion that he'd once loved her, he could be extremely dangerous.

During my drive to Montmorency, I couldn't help imagining how far he might go.

The venue was next to a burger bar at the top end of Were Street. Roots from huge gum trees had buckled the bitumen of the car park out the back, and my Honda thumped over ruts and humps as I steered into a nook in the far corner fringed with leafy native shrubs. A good position to observe from but not be noticed, if it came to it. However, I intended to pre-empt the subject and wait for her inside. Anybody looking for a tail expected them to follow, not lead.

Before alighting, I pulled out my mobile. 'Sit-rep?'

'The subject returned home twenty minutes ago. Hasn't surfaced since.'

Andre sounded excited, and it brought back memories of my first surveillance job, so I played it up for him. 'What else can you report?'

'Um.' He stopped, then I heard the snap of his fingers. *'She parked in the driveway—man, that's steep—not inside the attached double garage. I assume –'*

I tutted, and he corrected, *'Though it could be that the other car is in her way, this* might *mean she plans to go out again.'*

'Good.'

It was a Thursday, one of the nights she frequented Smokey Sax, and it would have been mighty disappointing if she'd stayed in. Of course, she'd already deviated from her usual routine by leaving the office late, so Andre could end up shadowing her to an entirely different location, leaving me to catch up.

I pondered on the other car, but never got the chance to ask.

After we'd disconnected, I extracted my key from the ignition. If I were Erica Vaucluse, served with divorce papers last week and a Supreme Court subpoena today, I'd definitely go to my happy place. And from the brief Kurt had provided, Smokey Sax was hers.

Today had been a good day so far, and I felt lucky. More fool me. So I went inside.

Despite its name, I wasn't expecting red brick walls, velvet curtains, chandeliers or ornately framed portraits of jazz greats on the ceiling. The retro microphone on centre-stage before a square parquetry dancefloor and the adjacent gleaming bar harking back to the Roaring Twenties also took me by surprise.

Who knew Monty had a joint like this?

When a stunning blonde in a silver-sequinned, floor-length dress slit up her thigh stepped up to the mike, the answer was quite a few people obviously did. They gave a round of enthusiastic applause, then she began. Her husky voice made the fine hairs on my forearm tickle as I settled myself in a booth in the back corner with an unhindered view of the room.

Andre phoned twice, the second to say, *'She's pulling into the car park now.'*

I became fidgety. Wished I had a martini, though I'd never drunk one in my life. Fiddled with the cocktail menu, then used it to conceal my eyes tracking Erica when she appeared, dressed as she'd been at the office. I hid my unease when she chose to sit at the round wooden table beside mine.

Andre followed about thirty seconds later. I stole glances at him, saw him pause and search for a woman in a wheelchair. After one sweep of the room, his gaze circled back to me. Impressive. Particularly as I had ditched BJ for the outing in favour of crutches hidden in the corner, switched to an after-5 outfit, freed my hair from its ponytail and brushed it over my right shoulder.

He'd changed too, trading jeans for black pants, short-sleeved shirt for a slim-fit, long-sleeved white-and-blue striped high-collar model, and he'd applied some product to his black hair. Good-looking in his daywear; eye-catching now. Nifty, because Erica was likely to take him for two different dudes.

Andre was halfway across the room when I gave another start. I recognised the dude behind him. But why was he here, and was it by chance or by arrangement? And was he aware of what Andre was up to? Or me?

The newcomer paid no heed to either of us. He covered the span from the entrance to Erica's table exuding an assertive personality with every stride.

I greeted Andre, who joined me on the cushioned booth seat. Holding a discreet finger to my lips, I covertly observed Erica.

Annoyance flashed over her face. 'You left the girls with the nanny?' She reached for her handbag, looking set to leave. 'Cannot believe you would encroach on my time-out.'

Her reaction struck me as somewhat affected.

Well, the lady is a lawyer. Poser by occupation.

'Let me buy you a drink, Erica.'

'Why would I do that?'

I indicated to the male and hissed to Andre, 'That's our client.' He widened his eyes.

Her husband said, 'A gesture to the past.'

Her answer was a sigh and a tight nod. She picked at the gold clasp on her bag until he returned with a pair of cocktails, soft pink under a layer of creamy foam.

'Pink Lady – you used to adore them, right?'

'I used to adore *you* too, William.' They took sips, each

watching the other over the rims of their glasses, then Erica added, 'But I don't see any of the qualities I loved about you now.'

His classy comeback was, 'Likewise.'

In their long, awkward pause, I asked Andre, 'So, was it tricky for you to get out tonight?' It didn't come across as nonchalantly as I'd hoped.

He smiled. 'No. Single and live alone. You?'

'Same. Not even a cat – I'm considering adopting one, though.'

We continued a disjointed and strangely revealing conversation in the frequent silences that punctuated the brittle, bitter exchange from the table next to us, until Erica gave an exasperated sigh. She turned away from her husband and our eyes connected briefly. I took a sharp breath at the close call. A second time, even minus BJ, and she might recollect our meeting earlier today.

I curved in towards Andre and whispered, 'Pretend we're making out.'

He shifted so our shoulders touched. His subtle scents of cinnamon and fresh linen were heady.

Softly, he said, 'Can you?' Even lower, he added, 'Make out?'

The rasp in his voice told me his question wasn't simple curiosity. We weren't faking here.

I gave a small nod. 'My legs are mostly numb and don't work, but I'm not dead at the waist.' Then I revealed something I'd never shared with anyone – always thought was a pipe dream. 'My specialists say I could have kids one day.'

His smile was as gentle as the fingertips he used to brush some strands off my face and tuck them behind my ear.

From my side-vision, I saw Erica slap the table top. The tea light candle between them fluttered, then extinguished.

'Why are you doing this? All this hostility?'

'It's not personal. Just business.'

Her 'Huh' cut through the sultry tones of the singer and murmurs around the club.

The couple dropped their voices and I couldn't make out what they said in the next few minutes. Then his mobile went, earning disapproving glances from patrons nearby.

'I need to take this, Erica. Wait…we have more to discuss.'

'I doubt it,' she bit back, but hung around while he moved well away.

Across the dancefloor, I watched him talk into his phone outside the gents' toilets. Assessing his body language, it seemed to be an intense conversation and that he'd be tied up for a while.

I focused on Andre. 'You know what I miss most?'

He shook his head.

'Dancing. I loved to dance before the accident.'

A light frown slithered over his face. Then he rose, and I went cold, embarrassed that I'd given away something so personal and he had nothing to say.

He came around in front of me. 'Trust me?'

He bent down. Understanding, I nodded. My arms looped his shoulders as his hands curled around each side of my waist. We lifted and came upright together, and slowly he lowered my feet to rest on the toe caps of his shoes. We swayed together in the small space near our booth, keeping Erica's back to us. For that minute or so, I was just a girl dancing with a sweet dude as the singer crooned a song about love and smiled at me across the dancefloor.

But then William pocketed his phone and he re-joined his wife. Both perched rigidly on their wooden chairs and I sensed one of them would leave shortly. I signalled Andre to the dark corner where I'd stashed my sticks and mouthed *Crutches*. Propped against our booth table, I locked my callipers, one hand gripping onto the table edge for support.

'*Sweet Baby's Eyes*,' Erica muttered. 'This was our song,

remember?' She got nothing in answer. 'Nowadays it would be *Sweet Baby's Lies*, wouldn't it, William?'

Again, no response.

'Back when we were happy, I let one thing slip about McLeod. You said nobody would ever know. And now you've used it against me?' She let out a huff. 'I need some air. But, it's my turn – wait, we have things to talk about.'

I didn't pick him as the type to do what he was told, but he did. He waited, and Andre and I tried to look nothing like we were waiting too. Full credit to us, we nailed the appearance of a couple making out, rather than two PIs on surveillance.

Three songs later, William glanced at his watch and stood up. While he did a scowling last check of the room, Andre and I left.

We'd reached my Honda in the dark nook of the car park ahead of our client stalking out of the club. I gazed around, searching for Erica. It didn't sit with me that she'd demand he wait and then leave. But the whole situation wasn't sitting with me anyway. I'd started to think Erica had predicted William would come. They'd both wanted a confrontation. So why not finish it?

I flicked my focus back to William, just as a woman emerged from the shadows in hot pants, slinky cami top, long black gloves and a brimmed hat. The redhead smoothed the sweeping fringe of her asymmetric bob with her left hand. By the way her chin tilted down, I gathered she felt wary of the dude lurking in the car park.

I reckon I'd guessed right, because she turned to a CCTV camera fixed high on the club's brick wall, and her air switched to assured.

She came abreast of William, and he was too busy checking out her bare legs to notice her right hand go to the band of her hot pants and then do a flick motion. My brain took a second to process what she held.

'HEY YOU! STOP!' As I yelled the words, she made a thrust to the side of William's neck.

By the time I'd managed, 'She's got a knife!' she had lunged it twice more, to his ribs and his armpit.

Andre and I were on the move. I was clacking along on my sticks and he loped ahead. But then he froze and gazed back at me. I sensed his male protective instinct had kicked in. He didn't want to leave me vulnerable.

What the hell?

I shouted, 'Andre! Help Vaucluse. Ring triple zero.'

He hesitated, then snapped into action. Meanwhile, the redhead had ditched the knife and now held a set of keys. The indicators flashed on a sedan reverse-parked two bays ahead. She was making a getaway.

I put on a surge.

As she cornered to the driver's side of the car, I thrust out my right stick. She lurched forward, the bunch of keys flying to clatter on the bitumen a few metres away. She held out her hands to cushion her fall, then thumped down, letting out a winded exhalation.

The impact of her tripping over my stick undid me. Fortunately, I spun to land on the bonnet of her car and kept a grip on both sticks. One was splayed across the car's front guard, the other slid, then found the ground. My legs tingled, gave a good spasm, but they couldn't hold me. My shoulders seared as they took my weight and I fought the pull downwards.

Andre's voice reached me—'...laboured breathing, massive blood loss...'—as I reeled and then heaved to right myself with my forearms, shoulders and stomach muscles all crying out, the crutches' cuffs cutting into the insides of my elbows, the handles crushing into the heels of my hands.

The redhead scrambled to rise. I gave her a knock with my stick, luckily only wobbling myself this time. She hit the deck again, but immediately curled and rolled to face the attack.

I shifted to lean on my left stick and drove the other one into her throat, pinning her down. She made a gasping sound.

Across the car park, Andre cried out, 'Hold on, man! BREATHE!'

Glancing over, I saw he'd wadded his shirt and pushed it to William's chest. Blood ran between his fingers. He could only address one wound. It left blood gushing from William's neck and starting to pool under his arm.

It didn't look good.

I must've pressed a bit too hard again because the redhead gagged. Then the fight drained out of her. Maybe the reality of what she'd done had sunk in.

I stared down at her. And then it clicked. I recognised those shoes. My eyes ran up to the tiny pants and top, both easily concealed under a business suit. To the bobbed hair, a bit too shiny and faultless.

Well, that explained the gloves and her desire to be caught on CCTV. With the costume masking her appearance and minimising DNA transfer, and using a different car, she might've gotten away with murder. Except she hadn't factored in Andre and me.

'Why'd you do it, Erica?'

Her eyes boggled, and I released some pressure.

'Had to.' She panted for breath. 'He would've ruined everything that mattered…my reputation, career, assets…'

A siren wailed in the distance and she slumped. I maintained my hold and dwelt on what she'd said for twenty seconds, then pointed out, 'You've done that yourself.'

There was more I wanted to say, especially about her kids not rating a mention in her list of what mattered and now growing up parentless. But I was sure she would victim-blame. And I might not control myself if she did.

My eyes returned to Andre, who was circled by onlookers, hands covering their mouths. He'd rocked back on his heels and stared at the blood-soaked material he clutched. He lifted his head, and in our passed look, something spurred him to lean forward and try to rouse William.

The siren grew closer, then silenced. White headlight spears illuminated the huddle, and flashing reds-and-blues from the cop car bounced off the building and parked cars. The engine cut, and two doors opened and shut.

One of the first responders waved his arms, driving back the spectators. His partner hurried to Andre and she nodded as he talked, while she checked William. Two paramedics soon joined them, but nobody rushed after that.

I dug my stick harder into Erica, so intent on her that a hand on my shoulder made me jolt and turn. She coughed as the force on her throat eased.

I faced Andre. He shook his head, and instinctively we drew together, his arms cradling my waist and the rapid thuds of his heart echoing between us. We trembled as one, adrenaline bleeding out as our client's life had done.

ABANDON

Winner Scarlet Stiletto Awards 2019
Special Commendation

ABANDON

A rifle shot split the sky as Chris Olden moved into the shade of the verandah. It was distant, and she barely noted it, concentrating on hauling open the front door.

She called out 'Hiya' in a general greeting and took a stool at the bar. 'Pot of Carlton. Ta, Dougie.'

The barman surveyed her as he pulled the beer. 'Hard day?'

'You could say that.' She paid, then raised her glass. 'Cheers.'

He nodded, flashed her a smile missing an eyetooth, and went off to rearrange the fridge.

Chris swallowed a mouthful and waited, hoping for a miracle burst of energy. She lost herself for a while, watching a pool game between two regulars.

She'd gone through school with these guys before their paths forked – uni for her, and stage one of succession plans for their family farms for them. They clunked balls in pockets giving cries that inflated their success, and bantered with Dougie's wife, Maura. But Chris saw chinks in their jollity – the regretful stretching out of a single beer, the wounded pride if someone offered a round because they couldn't return the favour.

Chris lifted her glass. Empty. She wasn't supposed to drink, but bought a second while a song about dusty gravel roads and leaving the past behind played in the background. She wondered whether moving forward was all it was cracked up to be. What if it turned out that her best years were in the past?

She took a gulp of her fresh beer, tasting sour hops and lost hope. Bloody country music; it did it to her every time.

A little low and keen not to show it, she took her pot out to the inaptly named beer garden. It was just an open space defined by an uncovered pergola lined with long tables and benches, their timber planks warped and split from numerous summers that set new annual records for the hottest and driest.

Nobody else was as stupid as Chris to sit out there in the blazing heat, swearing when the bare skin on the back of her thighs touched the timber. It suited her okay. One-quarter indigenous, her skin didn't burn, merely changed shades of brown, and she had things to think about without stopping to chat. Stuff her boss had said today to ponder.

Like maybe she'd be better off packing it in. Give up the fight to save the *Gazette*. Abandon Glory Valley – yep, this place was as incongruously named as Maura and Dougie's beer garden. The town shrinking and splintering, too.

The crack of a rifle went again, twice. The shots were still ricocheting off the craggy rocks on Hope Mountain when a third came. Chris shrugged. The sound had become more common in the past twelve months. Too many people around here were broke and hungry, and they supplemented what they could barter by butchering the stock they couldn't afford to feed and water, along with whatever game they could shoot.

A flush heated her face, nothing to do with temperature,

but all to do with shame. Here she was, contemplating the easier road. Leaving her old family home and becoming a townie. If she went, so would the paper – one of the last bastions of the glory days in Glory Valley. For a while, an overworked journo writing for the *Featherton Courier* would share their news. A paragraph or two in the regional paper. It might even be her; her editor had offered it. But before long, the paper would drop all pretence of interest in the unsophisticated blip of a town.

Chris had another thought. In a different place, would she wither or prosper? She suspected it'd go badly.

She took a slug and gagged on hot beer. She tipped out the rest and carried her glass inside. Left it on the counter and called out a general 'See ya.'

By the time she'd reached her ute, she was dragging her legs, craving a power nap behind the wheel. No chance with the air-con on the blink and the cabin twenty degrees hotter than the unstirring air outside. She cranked down the windows on both sides, then started up the engine. Movement would create a breeze. Might even wake her up.

She rubbed her hands over the stitched leather cover on the steering wheel. Her dad had insisted on getting it for her: good for grip and never too hot to touch. He'd been right about that…about most things.

The ute did a little skid on the dry gravel as she reversed and took off. Chris drove toward home wondering what her dad would've said about the things she had to decide on.

Easy to picture the look he would've given her and his laconic *Whatcha wanna do?* His advice would probably have been to follow her heart, her needs, like she had a choice. He probably would've then gazed out the window – didn't matter which window in the house, the view was the same. Across the valley to the hills, often tinged blue with eucalyptus haze. Always breathtaking, even when scorched and cracked in drought.

Her dad drifted from her mind as the tired ache from her lower limbs diffused upwards. It spread into her hands and shoulders, reached up her neck, banged away inside her head.

Still, hearing *'Please repeat that…'* she sat up straighter, and raised the volume on the police scanner.

'A body in the library. Male. Better send everything, but I don't think there's any urgency.'

Chris recognised the broad drawl of the second speaker: Paul Murchison. Another old schoolmate, and the cop in charge of their local station.

The D24 operator asked, *'Is the victim breathing?'*

'Not much chance of that with a hole straight through his throat.'

They went on for a minute without mentioning names while Chris whipped out a U-turn. Her headache increased as she considered the possibilities and backtracked, speeding past the pub and the rest of what constituted the CBD.

Their town didn't run to much in the way of full-time businesses apart from the pub, the small cop station, and petrol station-cum-general store – she even wrote a couple of weekly columns for the *Courier* while she wore virtually all hats for the *Gazette*. But a few generations ago, demand had exceeded supply of commercial space and a wealthy spinster bequeathed her double-fronted, two-storey Victorian home for use as a public library. Hugely popular, despite its isolated position on the outskirts of Glory Valley.

Four kilometres to go, and Chris was in conflict. For the valley, this story was huge. But it almost certainly involved people she knew, probably cared about.

Duty had to overrule sentiment. She kept driving and thinking.

With the decline in population and thus in members, the library had decreased its staff, trading hours, shelves and floor space, and rented out some of the spare rooms. It had two short-hour employees, and this wasn't one of the three days it opened, so she leaned towards one of the tenants as the victim.

She pulled up outside the old mansion within ten minutes of the radio call. Word had gotten around, and she'd been beaten by a cluster of locals. A crowd by valley standards. Eleven people at once.

Clambering from the ute, her body still ached. But she returned greetings and nodded when they hissed, 'So you heard?' In her mind, she started her breaking story.

A man's body has been found in Glory Valley Library.

She put it on pause as she edged in next to Paul. They exchanged 'G'day,' then he shook his head and muttered, 'Tommy Vawdrey. Why on earth…who'd wanna kill him, Chris?'

She took stock. The mortgage broker had flirted with everyone, any gender, any age, particularly if it might convert to business, but often just for fun. So she could easily name several current critics, particularly among the women he'd jilted and the men he'd encroached upon. But she mirrored Paul's disbelief. He really wanted to know who had marred his murder-free reign of the valley—someone they knew or an outsider—and why.

'Who'd have thought?' she said ambiguously, while recalling her dad's warning a few years ago: *Keep Tommy at arm's length – he'll come to no good.*

Chris refocused and asked Paul directly, 'What happened?'

He leaned in so nobody could overhear and told her, then watched over her shoulder as she took a photo through the window of what used to be the head librarian's domain, and of late acted as Tommy's office. The diamond-shaped leaded-panels—mostly green or red in colour, a few blue, some clear, and all with the waves and bubbles of old float glass—obscured the figure on the floor, and just before detectives and ambos arrived from Featherton, Paul approved her use of the image. Then she belted out a *breaking news* story to her editor that'd go straight online: concise, pure fact, no names or conjecture until Tommy's kin had been contacted.

On the way home, her imagination blazed with the opening of her follow-up.

With a permanent population of 506, major crime in Glory Valley tends to the occasional burglary, bar fight or illegal lighting of a fire, and its sole police officer, Senior Constable Paul Murchison, is generally occupied with traffic enforcement, domestics and collisions.

But today, this quiet town is in shock following its first murder in two decades…

It was only when Chris reached her empty house and looked out at the view her dad had loved, as she did, that she came down from her high. Exhausted and niggly throughout her body, she filed her story for the next morning, then collapsed without tea.

Ten hours later, she untangled herself from the sheets and rolled out of bed. Unrested. The oppressive overnight heat being least of her problems, though it probably exacerbated her symptoms.

She passed a hand over her eyes and sighed, coaching herself, 'C'mon, Chris. One foot in front of the other. People manage it. Stop feeling sorry for yourself. Just do it.'

Cringing, she muttered, 'A walking cliché. Not great for a journo.'

Talking to herself wasn't great, either, but she argued back. 'Yes, but that journo covered her first murder yesterday. And has been promised front page of the *Gazette* and *Courier*.'

Thinking of Tommy in the morgue, soon to be cut open, she winced.

After some minutes, and helped by strong coffee and a plateful of scrambled eggs and beans, a spark of energy came. It stayed while she rinsed the dishes, showered and dressed.

But as she was brushing her teeth, it drained down the hole with the minty water.

Hooking her toothbrush in the jar, she eyed the bottle of pills on the shelf above. Not a cure. A band-aid treatment. Untouched, so far.

She stared at the label, picturing her day ahead. From a long line of Oldens in the area, she needed to optimise her local status to gain an upper hand on the city press, who'd pay for stories or seduce with fleeting fame once they arrived. That meant interviewing a bunch of people, which involved partaking in one or more cuppas or beers at each place, yet staying switched on, firing at her best.

The time until tonight's candlelight vigil for Tommy would soon disappear.

Tiring to think about, it seemed impossible to achieve. Returning to bed grew tempting, but her dad's voice said inside her head, *So you're giving up?*

Maybe for today?

'No.'

The pills might restore some balance – or blur her mind. Chris ignored the prescription bottle and shook out two paracetamol. She washed them down with another cuppa, sitting out on the back deck with her legs dangling over the edge. She stared at the mountain, but her thoughts were with her dad. Wishing for the thousandth time he hadn't died, yet glad he never knew of her troubles. Only a doctor and a pharmacist in a town three hours from here did. She had to keep it that way. Had to prove to herself she wasn't washed up at thirty.

She got through the morning and afternoon, extracted some good quotes and background content, though she hadn't unearthed a star witness. Her editor raved over her latest story and her ideas for the next one. He promised to send a photographer across to capture the vigil.

'Unless they nab the bloke, it'll be old news next week,' he cautioned.

'Paul says they're a long way off solving this one.'

'That'd be right,' her editor grumbled, then hung up.

Chris let sleep take her. The phone rang what seemed like a minute later.

'I'm here.'

Bruno, her favourite *Courier* photographer. Old-school, he took pride in his work and respected a good journo. They'd clicked on their first assignment together.

She rubbed her eyes and strained to read the clock. She'd slept for an hour and the vigil would kick-off in twenty minutes. Crap.

'I'll be there asap.'

When Chris pulled into the main street, the long evening shadows from the mountain casting over the buildings looked other-worldly. The air was thick with dust and heat and hushed animation as she joined Bruno. They observed the swelling crowd carrying torches or mobile phones rather than candles, it being high-fire season, and then Bruno moved about, framing photos before he lost daylight.

More people filed in. The sun sunk lower and, though not necessary yet, torches went on. Chris followed the lead of cops and journos in movies, studying faces and body language. Most were dry-eyed. Some seemed to be enjoying the unusual event. None signalled guilt.

It was easy to pick out the press, homicide detectives and a handful of outsiders. The rest constituted most of the valley's population, many being those she'd interviewed that day.

She couldn't help doubting that every one of these locals was where they'd claimed to be when Tommy was shot. Sure, all but the pub was shut at the time. And the library sat out of town, with sprawling farms and empty cottages for immediate neighbours. But could the killer have stayed so measured they simply walked out the library gate and drove away without drawing any attention?

Someone covering up for family or a mate wouldn't surprise her. Gossip was one thing, but serious dobbing wasn't tolerated, not even to a journo or a copper born and bred here.

Chris swung her gaze over the crowd again. Paul Murchison stood with a bunch of police on the outer. Several regulars from the pub were grouped around Maura – presumably Dougie was keeping the place open for drinks afterwards. Senior residents took front positions. Chris's oldest friend, Ben Bao, hung to one side, with Chris's cousins, Joe Fegatello, and others of their era. Ben's ex, Ange, and her bestie were there too, but in a space by themselves. The generational divide, along with the absence of young families, hit Chris strongly.

The librarian, who also ran their hardware shop on the days the library didn't open and acted as the unofficial mayor in her spare time, lifted her hands.

'Thank you for coming tonight.' Her tone had an evangelistic ring. 'Tommy would be pleased.'

She went on and the murmur of her voice lulled Chris to the point where she stopped listening. Later, others shared a word or two, mostly about how the murder affected them.

Bruno joined Chris. 'I've got enough. You?'

She nodded.

'Drink?'

It was their tradition after covering a story together. But she couldn't, she needed bed.

Chris waved vaguely. 'Next time.'

He shrugged. 'No probs.'

She waited until Bruno's four-wheel drive disappeared, then dragged herself into her ute and steered it homewards.

'Drive and stay awake.'

She muttered the mantra continually, focused on getting

home, anticipating the serenity that always washed over her when she reached the five-acre parcel of scrub and modest cottage that'd been in her paternal family for four generations. Her little spot of paradise nestled among properties measured in hectares, neighbours few and far between. The place where she could let down her guard.

The minutes and kilometres stretched, and she repeated the mantra faster, anxious not to fall asleep.

Then Chris felt her head jerk. She came out of a doze and hauled the steering wheel to the left, the ute back into its lane, thankful for the otherwise empty road. The racing of her heart and bolt of adrenaline gradually declined.

Her mantra became, 'Nearly there. Nearly home.'

She took the last bend leading into the long straight to her place and stamped on the brakes.

'Not now!'

The ute's tyres skidded to a halt. Frowning at a fallen gum, she weighed two choices: deal with the roadblock or detour along Newfound Track.

She chose the easier option, doing a three-point turn and doubling back, then hanging a left. Away up the track, her headlights picked up a vehicle. It sat at an angle as if the driver had stopped in a hurry. It also sloped down.

She slowed on the approach, the twin points of her lights bouncing off the other car's windscreen and black bonnet. Drawing closer, she noted details. The BMW badge. That both tyres on the driver's side were flat. And she wondered at the dark blotch on the inside of the front window.

Her ute at a standstill, hazard lights on and nose-to-nose with the sedan, she'd already seen too much. A seething mass of flies and what she thought was a mist of blood spatter, with a slumped figure in the backdrop.

'Oh, shit.'

Chris grabbed her mobile phone and tumbled out of the ute, in a hurry to see if the person needed attention. She switched on the torch app and went to the driver's door. It sat ajar, had some blood smears on the edges. Wrapping her hand with the bottom of her shirt and avoiding the smears, she eased the door open, looked inside and gagged. There was no point except for formality, but she checked the man's vitals, fighting nausea, and then stepped back so fast she fell onto the rutted gravel.

Her hands were shaking so hard, it took both to hold her phone still enough to dial Paul Murchison's mobile. She stared up at a sprinkle of stars hanging in the sky above while listening to the rings.

'Hello? That you, Chris?' The words slurred. He'd had a few.

'Paul, I've found another one…' She flinched at a blast of background noise through the phone.

'What was that?'

'Another body…another gunshot victim.'

Chris crawled around to the front of the sedan while she waited for him to say something. He didn't.

'Paul? The man's behind the wheel of a new BMW.' She reeled off the registration number. 'I know the car, but…his face…he's not…I pretty sure, but…' The right words wouldn't come.

'Is this a joke?'

His flat tone told her he knew it wasn't.

'Is he alive?'

She shook her head for ten seconds before getting the answer out. 'No.' Feeling her head still wobbling, Chris gave him directions, adding, 'You'll see my ute – the hazards are on.'

He said something she didn't take in. Her mind was fuzzy with fatigue and shock.

'Make your calls now. I'll be here.' She hung up.

Two murders in two days in a town that rarely saw serious crime. If she was right about the car, and its owner was the latest victim, the man was Wolf Dortimer. He handled most of the real estate sales and auctions for the valley, though he lived and worked in Featherton.

She gazed at the shadowy countryside. Why was Wolf out here?

Shutting her eyes, she visualised the body inside the car. With no medical expertise, and with the heat and all those flies, she had no idea how long he'd been there. A few hours? A day? Longer?

Chris dragged out a memory. Yesterday, arriving at the pub after work, hearing one gunshot – clearly, that one killed Tommy. Then she'd sat outside with her second beer and noted more shots. She concentrated, remembered there were two in quick succession and guessed they blew out Wolf's tyres. The final shot would've been the fatal one that took off his face.

In the space between her drinks, the shooter must've driven from the library to Newfound Track.

Chris rubbed the raised nodules in her neck, wincing at the discomfort. Exhaustion tempted her to lie down and wait for Paul.

She fought off the desire. Instead, she shuffled around the BMW to snap some photos without disturbing the evidence and avoiding the gruesome money shots she could get big bucks for if she were made of more callous stuff.

It felt necessary to take a proper look at the body in the driver's seat. No mistaking Wolf's distinctive tri-gold wedding ring pinching in the flesh at the base of his finger or his pudgy knuckles. Likewise, the thick badger stripe of grey in his usually slicked-back jet hair. People often joked about why he didn't dye it, he could certainly afford to – but not funny now, flecked with blood and tissue.

Chris shuddered and, suddenly depleted, she staggered back to the ute. She perched on the tailgate and recorded her observations, writing her breaking story.

As two sirens came into earshot, she started on the follow-up: more colour, room for details to be added, and not for public consumption until the body had been ID'd and the family notified.

But the ghoulish anticipation of observing from the fringes and her hopes for a strong quote for the story were put paid by one of the out-of-town cops interviewing her, not Paul.

'I'll ask the questions, not you, eh?'

He smirked and slapped at a mozzie.

'Sure.'

She let him lead for a while, before having another try. 'Should we be worried?'

'What's that?'

'That there's a serial killer out here.'

The cop did a slow clap. 'You'd have to do better than that, love.'

But he didn't give her the chance. He wrapped up the interview and instructed her to contact Paul to formalise her statement tomorrow, then pointedly said, 'You can go now.'

Dismissed, there was still the problematic roadblock stopping her going home the usual way. And the driving need to make sense of things.

Why here? Why yesterday? Why Wolf? And was the killer done?

Chris drove the ute at little more than walking pace while she gazed about, thankful for the half-moon giving light to the landscape that constantly changed, but also stayed the same. Open, undulating paddocks, patches of scrub – all of it yellow and parched.

She continued onwards and pondered. The tree came down after she'd left for the vigil tonight, so Wolf wasn't using the track as a detour. So where was he travelling from the previous day? A local-access road, you'd only take it if your destination was one of the two properties coming off it.

Her thoughts circled to linking Tommy and Wolf. By local

standards, both were successful business operators, though the mortgage broker was outclassed by the real estate guy. Of a similar age, both tertiary-educated. One a player, inveterate bachelor. The other a family man, married with kids. No rumours had reached Chris about Wolf straying – or his wife.

A brain fog made her lose drift, before coming back to Newfound Track. It serviced two properties, but everyone used the main entrance when they went to the Jenkins farm.

So, there was only one place Wolf could've been returning from. And she was outside its front gate.

Chris stopped the ute. No sign of another car or movement, but she still had to check. She walked up the driveway, her attention shifting from the logo on the large *For Sale* board, Wolf's company name and his headshot, to the appearance of the old homestead.

No answer to her knock. No light inside the house, though the moon gave her a good view of the furnishings. Rented and professionally styled was her guess.

And then, with cold sinking from her chest to her toes, she knew. Not the full picture, not yet. But *enough*.

Back in the ute, she clung onto the steering wheel, letting the leather stitching press into her palms.

'Oh, mate.'

Heavy-hearted, she knew where to go.

She nosed the ute along a series of bumpy tracks, winding up Hope Mountain. During those fifteen or so minutes, dread built. Over the confrontation. What she might have to do.

Before she felt ready, Chris had arrived. Spotting the back end of another ute sticking out from some bushes, her eyes automatically went to its number plate. It had a banana bend, as she knew it would. It seemed unlikely that anyone was inside – but the past thirty hours made her doubt her instincts.

She looped around, glanced under the tarp covering the tray and through the dusty windows. Lots of junk, otherwise empty. Laying a tentative hand on the bonnet, she found it was cool. It'd been there a while. Chances were, since the vigil.

Chris turned away, drawn by the moon hanging low in the sky. Only half visible, but bright and enticing. It shone the way through a stomped down trail in the vegetation.

Years ago, two friends by the names of Olden and Bao, both young widowers with a child apiece, first brought their kids here. They taught them how to track, read a compass, a map and the weather. But mostly, how to be one with the land. To feel the spirit of everything around them: birds, animals, plants, rocks, creeks and natural forces. To be at ease with conversation, a book, or silence broken only by the sounds of nature. To be okay here, in the moment, even if nothing else in the world was.

A wave of longing for the old days made Chris pause. Her mum had died birthing her, and she missed Ben's dad almost as much as she missed her own – but thank God they didn't live to see this. Though if they were here…

No, nothing could change things.

She picked her way along the path. It grew more overhung as she neared the craggy ledge. She pushed aside arching branches, and saw Ben facing out, sitting on a flat-topped rock. Their rock.

'Hiya.'

He returned the greeting as Chris joined him. The ground seemed a long way down and she grunted with pain.

'Are you okay?'

Trust Ben. In a world of trouble, yet worried about her. Her problems weren't something she wanted to discuss. But then, he'd feel the same about his situation, only magnified.

For some minutes, they lightly banged their feet on the rock face, like they always had.

They'd always been honest, too, so she admitted, 'I've got chronic fatigue syndrome.'

He snapped a look at her. 'No shit?'

'Had it twelve months. Could go away one day. Could get worse.'

'You coping?'

Compared to him, yes. 'Yeah.'

She shrugged. They went back to banging their feet.

After a while, Ben said, 'Knew you'd work it out…just thought it'd take longer.'

'I saw Tommy in the library. Found Wolf in his car.'

He flinched. Swore softly.

'Went by your old place. It's been dolled up and put on the market again?'

Ben's chin jerked up. 'I'm a giant stuff-up, Chris.'

She swayed her head. 'We all make mistakes.'

'Not as massive as mine.'

She silently agreed, but diverted the subject. 'My dad always thought the world of you…so did I.'

Those last words held a wistfulness Chris hoped he'd missed. But Ben turned to her and she met his gaze. There was a question in his eyes, and she nodded.

'I never knew.' He gave a slow headshake. 'Thought you saw me as a big brother.'

She half-smiled. 'Just worked up the courage to say something when you fell for Ange…'

He reached for her hand and they clung on.

'I messed up everything, Chris. Couldn't make ends meet, borrowed even more money, lost the farm anyway, pushed Ange away. Dad'd be ashamed of me.'

She weighed her words before saying, 'Well, he wouldn't like what you did yesterday – but ashamed of you altogether, no.' After a minute's pause, she added, 'He'd be sad, Ben.'

They fell silent. Chris tuned into a slow, fluttery sound and watched a long-eared bat fly by in an unhurried rise and fall motion before sinking into a tree hollow. She wanted to hang onto this moment. Them sitting together quietly in their favourite place.

Too soon, Ben said, 'No way to fix what I'd messed up. But I could stop Tommy and Wolf preying on others.'

'There's been talk –'

'But nobody's ever *done* anything.'

She nodded.

'They were clever – Tommy sugar-coated, and Wolf steamrolled, if you know what I mean?'

'Yeah.'

'They were so slick, you didn't know you'd been done until afterwards. But by then you were in the shit and had to go back for more help…and they'd do you over again.'

She'd been halfway there when she saw the old farm and checked her understanding. 'They *helped* you out by buying the farm off you, but at a fire-sale price, just clearing the mortgage and leaving you nothing. They gave it a tart-up and were set to resell at a hefty profit, no doubt with Tommy financing the purchase, starting the cycle again, yeah?'

'Pretty much.' Ben sighed.

Slowly, methodically, he gave her all the specifics.

Chris kept thinking about drought, debt, depression – it had a way of ending badly. In heartbreak.

He scrambled up, facing her. 'You'll tell my story?'

Their gaze held.

She whispered, 'Of course,' wishing like anything it could end differently. Knowing better than to try to change it. Knowing he was already gone.

'You take care, Chris.'

Ben stepped towards the edge, opened his arms and dropped back.

She called out, 'I will!'

Her promise echoed off the rocks and floated down towards the valley, masking the sounds of his fall.

CHEESE, WINE AND THE PERFECT CRIME

First published in *The Victorian Writer*, October–November 2016 edition

CHEESE, WINE AND THE PERFECT CRIME

Cheese and red wine was a sublime combination. And a crackling log fire radiating its fingers of warmth through a room of wood, stone and iron perfected the scene.

The shiraz had legs – sexy legs. The runs on the inside of the wide-bellied glass drew the eye to the backdrop: a spreading puddle of red on the floor, between the hearth and black sheepskin rug. The texture was thicker, the red more rust-hued, than the wine that dribbled from the prostrate bottle still trembling on the flagstones. Next to the bottle lay a glass, also overturned, both somehow unbroken.

She let a swallow of wine weave its path over her tongue, coat her throat with dark berries and spices, then slide into her depths, leaving her mouth full of black pepper. A nibble from the wedge of bitey cheese merged with the aftertaste of the earthy wine and a unique metallic tang that hung in the air. It gave her a delicious shiver and she savoured it with another sip of wine, then admired the outline of her lips left in scarlet on the rim of her glass. The glass would leave with her, of course.

She laughed. The sound belonged in a smoky jazz club.

The fire popped, reminiscent of champagne corks and celebrations. Oh, he had made it dead easy for her. His fantasy of the noir woman—tight-belted trench coat, scarlet lipstick and stilettos, black suspenders and flimsy underwear—gave her the means for the perfect crime to match the cheese and wine. Black leather driving gloves, a trilby hat angled across her face and dark, Audrey Hepburn sunglasses, surprised him, thrilled him…and afforded her the flawless disguise.

The garb wasn't entirely necessary because she had been meticulous in arranging their secret rendezvous, equally so in ensuring there were no witnesses. But the wig, coat and rest of the costume also eliminated any chance of DNA or fingerprint transfer. There would be no links back to her.

In fact, there would be nothing to show anyone else had been in the cottage when he died.

Her long eyelashes fluttered, as she took another mouthful of the sinfully good wine and reflected. She had known what he couldn't resist in wine, woman and song. Just as she had memorised the exact layout of the cottage, well before she'd stepped one red-toed shoe inside it tonight. Chloe, her beautiful, naïve, baby sister, had shared everything from the moment she'd fallen in love with this debonair man, right up to when he'd broken her heart and taken her will to live.

The seven months since Chloe had ended her life afforded time to grieve, and time to plot the perfect revenge.

The man was clueless to being played, right up to the denouement. They were in a clinch, chest to breast, eyes locked, swaying and dipping to *Femme Fatale* by Nico, Reed and Cale. Timed with the line about playing him for a fool, she had tucked her ankle around his, grasped his suit lapel and flipped. His eyes had widened with realisation.

Impetus. The strength in her shapely calf and thigh. The angle of his fall if she thrust him away. The jagged edges on the stone fireplace… He was at her mercy.

She had whispered, 'This is for Chloe' and propelled him at the stone with just enough force to achieve her aim.

In keeping with the ultimate femme fatale—the killer woman—from his precious noir classics, she tipped back her glass, letting the last drips of delicious wine caress her senses, while revelling in her mission accomplished.

Death by accident, it really was the perfect crime.

THE WITNESS

Winner Scarlet Stiletto Awards 2017
Special Commendation

THE WITNESS

Legs slouched in the driver's seat, already bored with waiting around. He eyed off a kid who crossed in front of the car. He had a laptop sticking out of his bag and was plugging away at a Samsung mobile as he shuffled along in new Nike Airs. If Legs relieved the kid of his sneakers, mobile and computer, he'd flip an easy four hundred. Hungry for action, he reached for the door handle, then stopped himself and lit a smoke instead. They'd be up a few thou today if Bones pulled it off and she'd snap if he missed the pickup while he tossed the kid for small change.

The ute ahead with its hard tonneau cover and metallic gold duco looked brand new. A gap opened between Narelle and the Ford, but she could still make out a TIGERS decal on its rear window. Safe territory. Nothing to do with sex and his maybe/maybe not affair.

'Oh God, not even thirty seconds before you're back onto sex. Stop thinking!'

She fixed again on the Ford's window and breathed slowly, calmer until there was a flash of movement, and something—*an elbow?*—pressed against the glass. She squinted at the confused blur inside the cabin. The occupants were hugging or fighting. Stupid time to do either and it proved the world was full of idiots.

The Ford snaked on the road, slowing, and Narelle had to bang on her brake.

'What are you *doing*?' The valve on her anger released and she blasted the horn until the ute's left door opened and a girl flew out backwards. A tossed bag followed, then the ute roared away.

Narelle's mouth dropped when the girl rebounded off the side of a bus in the adjacent lane. She didn't move after hitting the bitumen and the bus kept going.

'What? No way!'

A car passed on the right, too, accelerating to get through the amber traffic light.

'You just drove past a person lying on the ground! Really?'

The girl twitched, then scrambled into a crouch. She waggled her head as if clearing a daze, snagged her backpack and rose, facing Narelle through the windscreen.

There shouldn't have been a hesitation. But instead of rushing to the girl's aid, Narelle took a sharp breath and checked her mirrors and the surrounding cars, mutely begging someone else to step in. Running on a sleep deficit, she was too tired to get involved. Her life was already enough of a mess without inviting in someone else's problems. As if to highlight that, her mind leapt to a series of alarming scenarios in rapid succession: the ute returning and the driver jumping out to attack them both; the girl getting in her car and turning psycho; the screech of tyres followed by a whiplash jerk as a car rammed them from behind when the light turned green.

Narelle jolted back to the moment. The now-red light meant she was a sitting duck and she clicked the central locking. She had under two minutes before the light switched to decide what to do. But then, she made eye contact with the girl who started limping towards her, the distress on her face making Narelle stab the unlock button. She couldn't leave her.

The girl read the signal and, with a glance in the direction the ute had taken, trotted faster than Narelle thought possible after what she'd been through. She must've been close to her daughter's age, and all Narelle could think was how she'd feel if it were her daughter thrown from a moving vehicle to hit the side of a bus that didn't bother to stop, and how appalled she'd be at a woman hesitant to help.

Shame coiled in her stomach as the girl reached the car and slipped into the passenger side, managing a gasping, 'Thank you.'

Narelle nodded, then honking from the car behind told her the light had turned. 'I'm going to lock us in.' She answered the girl's anxious glance with a smile. 'You're safe now.'

Instead of relaxing, the girl clutched the armrest. 'We need to get out of here before he comes back.'

Her fear overrode Narelle's instinct to call an ambulance. She turned forward and took off at a slow pace. There was every chance her passenger had whiplash and maybe a concussion. She was tall and slender, and Narelle didn't know if the lack of padding increased her chances of internal bleeding. Whatever her injuries, the girl must be in shock and needed medical attention.

Faking calm, she said, 'I'm Narelle and –'
Her passenger begged, 'Hurry! Please.'

'I'm going to call an ambulance, just to be safe. We'll wait there.' Narelle nudged her nose towards the petrol station ahead.

'No! Keep going!' The girl waved, panicky. 'There's nothing wrong with me. But if he comes back…' She covered her face and cried.

Legs kept checking his mobile. He should've heard from Bones by now. Her last SMS said she'd picked up a mark and should be at the location in ten minutes. Sometimes they had to do impro, and Bones was good, she hadn't fucked up yet. But Legs was getting a bad feeling. He revved the engine, ready to take off if she didn't get there in the next two minutes.

'She cried, so you brought her here?' Matt swept a hand around their lounge room.

Narelle shook her head, slitting her eyes at him. 'Keep your voice down.'

'What's wrong with you, anyway?'

He'd dropped his volume, but she wanted to slap the sneer off his face.

'With me?' She huffed. 'Nothing, except your midlife crisis.'

He stared at her, his expression flat. 'Who's having a midlife crisis here?' He turned left and right, as if searching for somebody, then faced her again. 'Oh, right, that would be the one who just brought a girl into our house, offered her our spare bedroom for as long as she likes, and gave her some of our daughter's clothes, wouldn't it? And all you know about her is that her name's Tia and she was run over by a bus.'

She snorted. 'Thrown out of a ute, then hit the side of a bus.'

He flung up his hands. '*Whatever*, Narelle.'

'She's scared and has nowhere else to go.'

Matt made the gesture of casting a fishing line and reeling it in. 'Hook, line and sinker.'

Anger seared her insides. 'Oh, you think I'm gullible?' He flinched and she went on, wishing she could yell, but keeping to a whisper. 'Good old Narelle. Too trusting. Easy to fool, huh?'

'For God's –'

She cut him off. 'I know what you've been up to.'

'Working hard for our family?'

Low and hard, she said, 'You and her.' Her lip curled. 'Annie.'

'*What?*' His nostrils flared. 'I won't even –'

'And bam.' Her laugh sounded bitter. 'There's the proof.' She held a palm to his face. 'You just lost the right to have an opinion about anything in this house. Go away and let me settle in Tia.'

Legs read the SMS while his free hand fisted. He thumped the wall, then kicked a bottle against a dumpster, glass smashing and spraying over the alley. Bones had gone too far this time. She was smokin' and insane, but screw her if this blew up in her face. She was on her own when it came to the cops.

Narelle's motives were warped, but not completely about showing Matt that she could be unpredictable and independent. Obviously, she couldn't drop Tia at a bus stop and hope she landed on her feet. The girl was on the run from a violent relationship, with no cash and ID because her boyfriend had stolen it before throwing her from the car, and her family had fragmented three years ago when her dad left them for his mistress and her mum took to drink.

With heartbreak over her cheating husband making her crave a drink so much that her hands trembled, Narelle could relate to Tia's family situation all too well.

She retrieved her mobile but hesitated, admitting bending over backwards to help Tia was a means of delaying the inevitable. Eventually, she'd have to deal with what Matt had done to their family. To her.

'Later.' With a grim smile in place, she dialled, waited and hearing it answered with, *'Sis,'* blew out a sigh. Talking to her big brother took the edge off almost as well as the whisky bottle, minus the hangover.

They small-talked for a few minutes, while Narelle shifted into the kitchen to prepare dinner. She covertly checked on Tia resting on the couch with her backpack pressed to her chest and her feet tucked under her bottom. Narelle was no doctor, but the girl's facial colour appeared good and though she occasionally rubbed at her thigh, Tia wasn't in obvious pain. She was also apparently unaware of the glares being directed at her from across the room.

Narelle waved Cass to the kitchen, but her daughter tipped her nose and went on staring at their guest.

There was background clattering over the phone line, then Paul said, *'I'd better go. Service is about to start.'*

'Wait up. The thing is,' she dropped her voice so the girls wouldn't hear, 'are you still looking for help?'

'Yeah.' He sounded wary. *'Do you want me to give Cass a go?'*

'No. God no. Never hire family, don't they say that?' She chuckled, panged at her disloyalty, then came to the point. 'No, but we've got a girl staying with us that could really do with a leg-up.'

Paul didn't hesitate, unlike Narelle at the accident scene, which made her feel guilty all over again. *'Sure, with you backing her, no probs. Bring her in tomorrow, sis.'*

After they disconnected, Narelle slid the roast into the oven and felt the first stirrings of doubt that she'd done the right thing in letting Tia into their lives.

Bones had sent another SMS while she was in the shitter. She couldn't talk but would ring later or message him. Legs chilled because what she said made sense. She'd been outplayed by the guy earlier, and he'd copped a good look at her, so she had to lay low for a few days before hitting the streets again. Anyway, she'd got lucky. The missus only had a lame runabout but her old man had a classy Audi, and their kid had more gadgets than the bitch deserved, and there'd be a stash of cash in the place somewhere, so Bones saw a nice little earner while she was being treated like a princess. And by the time she was done, she'd have worked out how to score the Audi.

As Narelle added the vegies to the roasting pan, Cass finally joined her in the kitchen. But her crossed arms signalled she was only there to pick a fight.

'Why'd you bring her here?'

Cass's best snarky tone never failed to get up Narelle's

nose, but she pictured Matt doing his fishing impersonation and breathed instead of snapping back.

Her daughter's face slackened, clearly disappointed she hadn't scored a hit, then she lifted her chin and tried firing from another angle. 'You never got *me* a job with Uncle Paul.'

Narelle ignored that too; it was old ground rehashed. 'She needs our help, Cass. You've got me and Dad, but Tia's got nobody.'

Cass sniffed. 'Have I?'

'Have you what?' Narelle sighed. She could do with some peace and quiet instead of her daughter's attitude.

'You and Dad are splitting, aren't you?' Cass jammed her hands on her hips.

Were they splitting up? It depended on whether Matt was a lying, cheating scumbag, which seemed likely. They had to talk. Really talk. Even if he wasn't having an affair, he wasn't invested in their marriage. So, either way, he wasn't being truthful, but their daughter deserved honesty now.

'Hon, I don't know.' Narelle reached out.

Cass shrugged her off. 'Well, if she's staying, I'm going.' Slyness glazed her eyes. 'Me and Dad'll get our own place.'

Legs had a boner and wished Bones was there to help him out. He laughed out loud thinking about the double-meaning of Bones's nickname: boner-causing, and tall and leggy. Though she stood about five centimetres taller than him, he couldn't call her Leggy because he'd been Legs first; he'd gotten the name for being fast and good at dodging cops. Legs got to thinking about her curves in the right places and his boner throbbed. He was bunked and needed a release and this was only day one. After a suck on his bong, he sent Bones a pic of his hard-on.

Cass had scored well: ten out of ten on the Bitchter Scale. But Narelle wasn't going to show how much she was hurting. She pasted on a smile, pulled open the top drawer and grabbed handfuls of cutlery.

The corners of her mouth slipped when the front door banged. Cass had stomped upstairs, so it had to be Matt.

She muttered, 'Awesomeness.'

'Relle?'

He hadn't called her that in ages. She ignored him.

Matt's voice was closer when he said, 'Could we stretch dinner to one more? I've brought a friend for you to meet.'

She nearly lost it. Nearly screamed at him that he wasn't welcome, let alone any friend. But then Narelle glimpsed the woman behind Matt, as he said, 'Relle, this is Annie.'

Annie. In her kitchen. But not the young, sexy version Narelle had envisaged. The real Annie wore her grey hair in a shaggy bob and a smart pants suit over a figure as wide as it was tall, which was sub-five-foot.

Matt came alongside Narelle. 'I should've done this sooner. We've been spending a lot of time together because Annie's top-notch at people skills, which isn't always my forte.' He grimaced and Narelle supposed it was meant as an apology. 'She's the best judge of character in our office. But she's not techno-minded –'

'To put it kindly.' Annie smiled, her face creasing with laughter lines.

'So, I've been helping her set up processes that she can manage.'

'Win-win,' Annie said. 'Except that I've been keeping your fabulous husband away from home too much.'

Ashamed that she'd misjudged the situation, heat bloomed on Narelle's cheeks. She rushed to say, 'It's lovely to meet you, Annie. We've got plenty of food. Matt, can you fix some drinks?'

He shot her a grateful smile just as Cass appeared and started chatting with Annie. Narelle's eyebrows lifted when she heard her daughter giggle at something the older woman said, considering it'd be nice if that civil side extended to her own mum.

Then, seeing Tia hang back, not even breaking through her shyness when Annie sat next to her on the couch, Narelle frowned, concerned. But Matt distracted her by dropping a kiss on her neck and Narelle wasn't sure if she was more surprised by the gesture or her instantly weak knees.

Tia's voice made her turn quickly. 'I'm tired. Would you mind if I have something to eat in bed?'

'Of course not.' Narelle grasped her mobile. 'And I'll call a doctor out.'

'No!'

Narelle flinched.

'Sorry. I'm good, just tired. I told you before that I don't need a doctor.' After a pause, Tia added, 'Thanks though.' She smiled and with arms wrapped around her bag, nodded goodnight.

Turning back to the stove, Narelle caught Annie watching Tia leave with her head tilted and a small furrow on her brow. Unease brushed over Narelle again, but she pushed it aside and threw beans into the steamer.

He laughed so hard he rolled sideways off the bed. Bones whispered, *'It's all so nice and suburban here that I want to stick my fingers down my throat and vomit all over them.'* Then she told him about an old bag that'd come for tea. She'd freaked Bones for some reason and Legs stopped laughing.

'Are we good, Relle?'

Matt lay on his side, facing her in the soft glow from her bedside lamp. His eyes begged and she wanted to say yes. But meeting Annie and an enjoyable night together hadn't resolved everything.

'Today was a start, Matt.'

He curled closer and twined his legs with hers. It was nice, but she pulled back when he stroked her hip.

He looked hurt, so she whispered, 'Just hold me tonight, okay?'

Matt nodded and moulded his body to hers. When his cheek dropped against her shoulder, she knew he was asleep. But the roller-coaster day kept her wide awake after clicking off the light.

Her mind darted between how she and Matt could repair their rift, worries for Cass's final SACs and exams, and their houseguest. Tomorrow, somehow, she'd get the girl checked by a doctor, and as much as the idea clearly frightened Tia, she had to report her attack to the police. Throwing a girl out of a moving vehicle was not on. Nor was stealing all her possessions and intimidating her into silence.

Narelle frowned at the ceiling, listening to Matt's soft breaths. If the ute driver had stolen all of Tia's things, what was in the backpack that she never let out of her grip?

Legs couldn't sleep. The fuck was that about? He'd grown soft, that's what. Maybe he needed to give Bones the flick and go solo again. It wasn't like they were in coupledom, right? And he'd never had a problem looking after Number One and keeping business and pleasure separate before Bones. He'd

**pick up some booty when the urge came, hump 'em
and dump 'em. He rolled over and checked his
mobile, but she hadn't gotten back to him yet. He
sent another message: 'bail – not worth it'.**

Narelle jolted awake, so she'd dropped off at some point. But her limbs and eyelids weighed a tonne, a sign that she'd spent mere minutes asleep out of the six hours they'd been in bed.

She groaned, then tuned in to Scamp, puzzling over why he was scrabbling near the door. He was a wonder dog, able to snooze for nine hours without a wee break and when he needed to go outside, he gave a short bark and held on until someone let him out. He didn't scratch at the floorboards or get agitated.

Not a stir from Matt. She'd never admit it aloud, but she hated his ability to sleep so solidly. With no hope from that department, Narelle trundled out of bed and dropped next to the beagle.

'What's up, Scampie?'

He snuffled her hand, then clawed at the bottom of the door.

'Is someone out there?'

He cocked his head in both directions. The question wasn't in his vocabulary. But something was amiss.

Narelle eased open the door and Scamp shot away. He raced up the hallway, then the tapping of his toenails faded as he scampered down the stairs.

When he started braying, the hairs on Narelle's nape prickled. She snatched up one of Cass's shoes from where she'd kicked them off in the hallway, and held it up as she descended the stairs on tiptoe, freezing for a second at the squeaky tread midway.

She hugged the wall as Scamp's barks amplified. Rounding the corner into the lounge room, she almost collided with someone, yelped and jumped back, dropping the shoe.

Frowning, she gaped at Tia. Dressed in Cass's clothes. Holding her backpack – it bulged.

'Sorry, did I wake you?'

Scamp went quiet and edged next to Narelle, pressing his flank against her leg.

Tia spoke again. 'I wanted to be ready early…for the interview with your brother, yeah?' She followed Narelle's gaze, which was glued to the bag. 'I borrowed a couple of books. Hope that's okay?'

Legs waited where she'd told him to go, but she was a no-show. Again. What was he, a fucking taxi? He went from pissed to churning with dread. Maybe she'd been nicked and was being pushed around by the cops. She wouldn't crack. Would she? His bowels cramped when he thought about what she knew. If she spilled, they'd both be screwed.

For all her eagerness to be ready for her interview with Paul, Tia acted less than keen when they reached the restaurant. It could've been nerves. But Narelle's doubts about the girl grew during the meeting.

She stared at Tia, reflecting: no money, ID, phone or work references. A dysfunctional family, a violent boyfriend, and a scared and lonely girl.

Or an inventive liar?

'Right.' Paul slapped his thighs and rose. 'Let's give you a tour and introduce you around.'

Tia's feet dragged as she followed him. Narelle immediately scooted to Paul's computer on his desk. She was on the internet in seconds and searched *Tia Cookson*. She scanned the hits, then went through the images Google found. Rueing her slow pace, she eliminated everything on page one. Half the results on page two related to transient ischaemic attacks, transportation or foreign registers with the initials *TIA* or the name *Cookson*. The other hits bombed too. By the third page, Narelle decided the girl was using an alias. What teen wasn't on social media?

She broke into a nervous sweat and banged out a fresh search, determined to unmask Tia.

'Who are you really?'

She hit a wall on the missing person registers, realising they only listed those gone long-term. And searching other sites without the girl's real name would be difficult. In fact, impossible if nobody had reported her missing.

And Tia and Paul might be back soon. Narelle was running out of time. She went to the Crime Stoppers site and pulled up Wanted Persons.

'Better.'

At least she now had names, images and descriptions of alleged offenders and their crimes. She scrolled through some. It would take too long unless she narrowed the results. She filtered using *female*, but for some reason it came up with one male, then tried a few other angles, starting to doubt she'd find Tia there. The girl claimed to be nearly seventeen; as a minor, would her details be publicised? Besides, she might be dodgy, but not criminal.

Narelle ran out of steam. She slumped so her forehead rested on Paul's desk.

Bones had planned to roll this morning, then got caught by the missus. She'd bluffed her way out of it, but couldn't ditch the poxy job interview. As if she'd work in some kitchen when what they did paid heaps better. Joke, right? But now Bones wanted to stay in with the family until she'd knocked off some more gear and worked out a plan for the Audi. It might mean another day or so stuck in suburbia though, and Legs didn't like Bones playing at something they hadn't planned properly. He kicked the bin, upending it, scattering rubbish over the floor. It didn't help his frustration or his nerves. He needed a cone to chill.

Tia rubbed her temple, pulling one of the *I'm too sick for school* expressions that Cass occasionally used. Narelle held back, sceptical, but Paul immediately assured her, 'There's no rush to start. Rest up for as long as you need. Just let me know when you're good to go.'

'Thanks.' The girl produced a wan smile.

And *that* handed Narelle the ammunition she needed to get Tia to their family doctor. Frustratingly, not being a parent or guardian, she wasn't allowed to be present for the consultation or be privy to details except Tia's summary, 'Doc said I was lucky; there's nothing wrong that rest won't fix,' though the receptionist had no qualms about handing Narelle the bill. But, no amount of cajoling or pressurising could get the girl to talk to the police, so Narelle drove them home.

With an exaggerated sigh, Tia shuffled inside and stretched out on the couch using her backpack as a pillow, which blew the idea of searching it if the girl fell asleep. Narelle itched to continue her hunt for Tia's real identity, but didn't dare do it in the same room. Claiming a headache, she shut herself in the bedroom with her iPad.

As she chewed her lip and pondered what to enter in the search field, the door flew open.

'Mum! Where's my iPod? And I can't find my Fitbit! What *the*?' Cass rolled her eyes, didn't wait for a response, and exited.

Narelle guessed where Cass's gadgets were. But guessing was a far cry from proof. Perched on the bed, she contemplated the ute and what she thought she'd witnessed, then reversed it, typing *teenage female car theft assault Wantirna*. Then she decided Wantirna was too specific because offenders would move around to avoid being caught, and broadened the search to Melbourne.

Lots of hits. Some mentioned the Apex gang. Others, mobs of teenagers. Everywhere from the western suburbs, to inner city, bayside, and satellite cities in the east. Because Tia had been alone with the ute driver, Narelle focused on incidents involving one or two offenders, landing on the report of a carjacking of an Audi matching Matt's. Her eyebrows hoisted, but scrolling further, she dismissed it.

After a pause, she went back by two clicks and squinted at a screenshot of a *breaking news* story on the *Sunrise* TV program last year. In the foreground were an unmarked police car and a patrol car with a huddle of plain clothed and uniformed cops. Between them and a throng of bystanders was the carcass of a smashed sedan. Narelle narrowed in on a figure who stood apart from the crowd.

'Tia…or whoever you are!'

Galvanised, she clicked through more images, until she stopped at the headline, *Teenager wanted over violent carjacking in Melbourne's west*, with Tia's image, though the report referred to her as Tanya Caulfield, aged nineteen.

Bones couldn't talk because the missus was acting weird as, but she messaged all the deets. She'd grab what she'd stashed in the wheelie bin and whatever she could fit in her bag and meet him at the location at 1.00am. She'd come up with a plan for the Audi too, though Legs wanted to stick at what they were good at: jackings. Most men couldn't drive past Bones 'in distress' on the roadside, and picturing their faces when she pulled out her knife and a syringe filled with his blood cracked Legs up every time. In this case, the mark would recognise her, so she'd nicked a spare key thinking they'd leave it a few weeks, then take the Audi from outside his office. Changing their MO made Legs edgy. Maybe he could talk her out of it. She'd probably tell him he was a soft cock for being worried.

Narelle decided Matt couldn't have been more wrong about her. She might be kind-hearted, but wasn't gullible, and she appeared to have a knack for underhandedness. She smiled at Tia/Tanya across the dining table. The girl had no idea what was coming.

Scamp nuzzled Narelle's hand and she scratched his head. They were the modern-day Scooby-Doo and Shaggy. He'd provided a decoy for her to do the detecting. She'd teased him in the garden with his favourite rubber bone and then put it just out of his reach, as if he'd flung it in the air a bit too energetically. His commotion drew everyone out of the house, while she ducked back in.

For three precious minutes, she'd had access to Tanya's backpack. Wearing disposable gloves, Narelle had rummaged through the bag, unsurprised to see it crammed with most of their portable valuables, including Matt's spare key fob, her engagement ring, and the emergency money from the flour tin. She'd also found Tanya's purse, with ID intact, a wad of cash and a bunch of strangers' credit cards.

And a mobile phone.

Legs was hyped. Bones had just rounded the corner, with her backpack and a stuffed garbage bag banging behind her. He'd half expected something to go wrong. She wouldn't show, nicked by the cops or bailed up by the dumb dog again. But it couldn't have gone better. She'd picked a quiet street; the houses were in darkness and too average to have CCTV or anything. Legs twisted out of the car, glad Bones had reminded him to disable the interior light, and moved to meet her.

The one condition Narelle had attached with her tip-off was that she be allowed to watch the police take down Tanya and her accomplice, though they'd pointed her to a position further away than she liked and her buzz dwindled after standing still for an hour.

But finally, she saw a tall, shadowy figure meet another, even taller one. Her breath caught when car headlights suddenly beamed white light, catching Tanya pass her backpack to a male youth.

'HOLD IT! POLICE! Hands in the air!'

Tanya screamed abuse as she followed the male, sprinting for a gap in the ring of police primed with torches and tasers. She took the lead just as a cop filled the space and she collided with his broad uniformed chest. Sprawling airborne as she had after hitting the bus, her legs tangled with her accomplice, felling them both to the gutter.

As the police snapped on handcuffs, Narelle chuckled, nudging Matt in the ribs.

He leaned in and whispered, 'Look at you, Relle. You got them – hook, line and sinker.'

BALL AND CHAIN

Winner Scarlet Stiletto Awards 2014
Great Film Idea Prize

First published in *Scarlet Stiletto: The Sixth Cut – 2014*

BALL AND CHAIN

A woman screamed in staccato bursts. The eerie sound ricocheted off trunks of gumtrees, ghostly yet grand in the moonlight and stirred sentinel owls among the branches. The rhythm of *woo, woo, woo* increased as the owls spread their alarm.

The fluorocarbon strand under the pads of Jess's fingers quivered. She tensed and peered into the shadows.

The line beneath her fingers had stilled by the time the shrieks resumed. These longer cries were answered in the distance somewhere to her left. Jess tilted her head, closing her eyes to concentrate.

Over the years, the mating calls of red foxes and human screams seemed to merge. Likewise, pops that could be gunshots were waved off as backfires, while windows broke and car panels dented, yet were just accidents. Black eyes and broken teeth were harder to ignore, but self-preservation, fear or apathy were as debilitating and pervasive in this town as arthritis in old bones.

The lucky and strong moved away and soon ceased fighting for those left behind. The rest didn't have choices, opportunities or strength to escape, and dragged the ball-and-chain of financial dependency, constraints of family or jobs.

Jess's rod jolted as the line tugged under her fingertips again. She opened her eyes and focused on the float ten metres in front. It bobbed, once, twice, then submerged. She jerked the rod upwards. The human-slash-fox screams fused with thrashes of the hooked fish. Jess landed her catch, wondering what she'd do if she knew the shrieks were human.

She eyed the pretty trout; it'd be a good feed. Then she thwacked its head with her metal donga and threw it into the bucket. It splattered her with blood and water as it lashed around.

When the trout's death throes ended, she noticed the shrieks had also stopped and even the owls had silenced. That seemed scarier than ever. But not as chilling as the realisation that Jess had equal chances of leaving town and being able to defend another person.

None.

The truth depressed her, so she didn't replenish her hook but sat on her favourite log, staring ahead. Gradually, the sun and moon tagged, and Jess roused from her trance, stretching the stiffness from her body.

She gathered her fishing gear and passed the ranger as she headed for home. A lifted chin and small quirk of the corners of their mouths accompanied her 'Morning' and his reply, 'G'day'.

The ranger didn't check her catch but eyed the stick in her right hand, as he did most days. He was an advocate of users taking everything they brought into the park and nothing more; his disapproval of her habitual removal of a long stick was clear. But he also knew she wasn't one of the bad ones, which was probably why he let her get away with it.

When Jess reached the front door to the cottage, she tossed the branch over the balustrade onto a growing heap. The smack and rasp of sticks as the stack resettled grated on her nerves. The branches made good kindling but even during the last cold snap, she'd shunned the pile unless desperate, then handled it like a contagion.

That day followed her usual routine, most of it sleeping when people normally worked. And at eight in the evening, she pulled her van into the driveway of a factory in darkness, to work when most others played. A minute later, Jess unbolted the padlock to the roller door from inside. A chunky chain ground on the wheel as she manually hoisted the shutter. Metal scraped and banged but the sound wasn't as jarring as the sticks hitting the pile each morning.

Jess read the note on the clipboard hanging above the main light switch, then loaded up. But just as she pushed a drum of contact adhesive into place, a numbness struck her from toes to chest. She waited it out and eventually managed to finish off at the factory, climb up into the van and operate its foot pedals.

At the nearby community centre, Jess caught a glimpse of a ute in the car park. Her stomach dropped, and she quickly steered to the rear entrance. There she stared at the yellow brick building, dreading the night ahead.

The ute she'd dodged was a bogan job. The white Holden's brutal bull bar sprouted antennas the size of surf fishing rods and a row of spotlights mounted on the roof pointed front and back. A RM Williams longhorn sticker covered the rear window and decals of big-jugged girls wearing nothing more than stilettos or g-strings overlaid every other bit of glass, with the odd boy pissing on a Ford for a touch of class.

A canary-yellow job inevitably flanked the white ute, with bigger and better spotties and four-inch-thick chrome upright exhaust stacks behind the cabin. And if it wasn't obscured by the other two cars, Jess knew a third ute would soon roll up. Midnight blue, it was less redneck than its counterparts, aside from the mural of a naked woman spanning the bonnet and the triple air horns on its roof.

The utes weren't the problem, though. Bile coated her throat at the thought of the thick-necked, loud-mouthed bullies who drove them too hard, fast, loud and drunk.

She sighed, making her chest balloon then deflate. Procrastination wouldn't get the job done, and her boss paid by the cupboard not the hour. As she jumped down from the van, she told herself to ignore the hoons and hoped they'd do likewise.

Jess hauled out the truck trolley, loaded up the first whiteboard carcass and wheeled the box to the back entrance. Though the door was locked, the building wasn't armed, but she wasn't surprised. The ute-bogans had keys and access codes to anywhere that mattered in town.

She bumped the trolley over the entry mat and cringed as the tyres squealed on the linoleum floor. Jess pushed faster, but the message malfunctioned between her brain and left leg, causing her to stagger. Luckily, she caught the thud of a ball and squeak of sneakers on timber coming from the middle court. The bullies were obviously engrossed in a basketball game. She made it unmolested to the office she was fitting out and expelled the breath she'd held.

Jess trekked to and from her van, while the game on centre court continued. She whistled softly as she marked a kicker for scribing to the drop in the floor but delayed dragging out the electric planer. Its shrill buzz had set off a chain of dogs last night. Once she turned it on, it'd broadcast she was in the building as clearly as a message over the loudspeaker.

And everybody knew she worked alone.

Jess liked working alone. It suited her personality and lately, it suited her situation. Her boss was happy with the setup, knowing she didn't need micromanaging and was more productive on her own than his two thickhead sons combined. That meant she did more installing than construction nowadays, but with the town's steady decline, creative jobs had become rare, and cheap, functional work the norm, so there was more challenge in fitting most of the projects than banging together white boxes in the factory.

The stack of marked kickers had grown, and Jess needed to move along. She plugged in the planer, then froze.

Her pulse rocketed as she waited for the noise to repeat. It hadn't sounded like harmless play on a basketball court. And she was certain it wasn't the foxes that slunk along the aqueduct behind the community centre. It was also quite different to what she'd heard when fishing last night.

Still waiting, she noticed that the ballgame had stopped. Slow handclaps, jeers and laughter, along with the chink of bottles, were dulled by the thick walls enclosing the indoor court, yet unmistakable. Her stomach shrivelled as her imagination filled with jerks and violence fuelled by alcohol. The sound of shattering glass boosted her alarm.

Then the noise came again.

'Oh, God.' Jess fumbled with the planer and stuffed a hand over her mouth.

The sound was haunting, thick with panic, and it triggered lightning strikes inside her body. Her nerves pulsated. Randomly. Painfully.

As the screeches amplified, Jess's eyes blurred and throbbed. Overloaded by fear, her body was shutting down. Her phone was about a metre away, on top of the toolbox. But who could she call? The cops were the ones she needed to stop. Other locals with authority were related to them either by blood or type. And nobody else would risk turning up at the centre and taking them on.

She aimed for the exit, but every movement lagged. She finally reached the door, snapped the lock and flicked off the light switch. It sickened her, but she had to think first of herself and hope the poor person out there got away with repairable physical injuries. Psychological damage was already a given.

Her legs crumpled, and she leaned against the wall, heart thudding, mind processing.

So far, the men were unaware of her presence. They would've been in to harass her earlier if they'd realised.

They mightn't notice her van, as she'd parked behind the building, whereas their utes were out in the main lot. But if they did spot the van, they'd recognise it as hers. As she'd been progressively refurbishing the offices after-hours, they'd know she was inside the centre, if not which room she worked in.

She just hoped she hadn't left scuffmarks on the lino from the trolley or transferred sawdust from the van that'd lead them to her hiding place.

Shivers made her teeth chatter. Fearful the noise would give her away, Jess compressed her jaw. A shout preceded a bang. A door hitting something, she thought. The sound of running feet and angry yells escalated, then faded.

Jess squeezed her eyes shut, her jaw still clamped. She was a goner. They'd run past her door, so they must've been headed for the rear exit. There was no way they'd miss her van.

On the upside, it seemed that the person being tormented had gotten away. *Good on them.* That meant they were mobile. She hadn't thought it possible judging by the shocking noises coming from the gym.

'Oh, Jess!' The call came in a singsong tone.

A different voice called in similar sugary-sweet pitch, 'Jess Weldon, we know you're here.'

Thuds echoed through the building. Fists or feet banging on doors or walls, she guessed.

'Weldon.' The rough gravel tone of this speaker belonged to the white ute bogan – the sergeant and officer-in-charge at the local cop shop, Craig Barclay, known as 'Barca'. 'Come out. Come out. Wherever you are.'

A thump on the wall close to Jess's head made her gasp. Thankfully, her giveaway was lost in the commotion. The men's sporadic blows sped up and were repeated in time with the quick thuds of her heartbeat.

'Oh, Jess.' Barca's younger brother and 2IC at the station, Simon, still chanted singsong style. She knew he wouldn't keep it up. Simo would revert to type and grow more threatening as he became frustrated. Hate would steam out of him like fumes from his yellow ute's exhaust stacks.

'Jessie. Come out and play.' That was Hodgey, also using a fake-friendly tone. Tim Hodge was bottom of the tier at the station at constable level and might've been a nice guy if he hadn't become matey with the Barclay brothers. These days, he was as rotten as the other two.

'Has the cat got your tongue?' Simo's nasty side emerged. 'You turned dumb like your *retard* dad?'

Jess's hands scrunched into bony balls as she controlled her anger.

Barca yelled, 'Get out here. Now!'

Inside her overalls pocket, Jess's fingers found a key. Her fingertips traced the jags on its blade. She hoped the manager hadn't lied when he'd explained that, though the external doors and basketball courts were keyed alike, every office and storage area had a unique lock, and he was the only person with access to the master key. He'd issued her with a fresh key as she worked her way through the office renovation, trading the one belonging to the room she'd just completed for the next on her list. Each time, he'd checked, *You haven't let this out of your sight, have you, young Jess?* and she'd replied, *Of course not.*

She had an inkling now why it'd been so important to him. He couldn't keep Barca's gang out of the centre, but he could try to protect the offices and storerooms.

'You might as well come out, Weldon,' Simo crooned. 'You have to *come out* sometime.'

The men laughed; cruel, crude cackles.

'We can fix you, you know, dyke.' Barca again.

'Yeah, all you need is a real man.' Hodgey whooped.

They thought she was a lesbian because she was female, did a 'man's job' being on the tools in cabinetmaking and was definitely uninterested in anything they had to offer. They'd molested her physically and verbally for years but hadn't beaten down the defiance in her eyes. She knew that annoyed and egged them on, but she had to stand up to them somehow.

Well, she'd have to come out of the closet soon; her symptoms were worsening and the signs harder to hide because of the extended heatwave. *Not yet.* She had things to do, arrangements to make first.

Tonight, she'd wait them out because, unlike Barca's gang, she had patience. She could cower in here all night, while they'd quickly lose interest and move onto something more instantly satisfying. As soon as they did, she'd bolt. It'd delay the project, but she bet the manager would understand when he saw the mess.

For the next half-hour, Jess stayed on tenterhooks and tried to ignore the curses, taunts and noisy destruction of the building. One part of her found black humour. She'd have heaps more work here. By the sounds of it, she'd have to revamp reception and replace the display cabinets along the corridors. She just hoped the centre could keep its doors open in the meantime. The activities it ran were about the only bright side to a shitty life for most locals.

Finally, Barca yelled, 'You'll keep, dyke.'

His brother, Simo added, 'Sweet dreams.'

Jess heard distant car engines fire, the squeal of tyres doing doughnuts, then silence. Perfect quiet. Except for the booming pulse in her ears.

For a time, she didn't move. She breathed, steadying her heart rate, supplying oxygen to her muscles in the hope they'd do what she needed when asked.

Once she felt a little stronger, she rang the centre manager and told him what had happened. He cried, then thanked her, which was even more pitiful. After removing her personal gear, Jess secured the office, picked her way through the carnage and locked the front door. She returned to the rear of the building, set the alarm and exited. The manager would shed a thousand more tears before lunchtime tomorrow.

Jess went home but didn't go inside. Routine was essential. So she walked to the lake, brushed bird poo off her log and sat. But she didn't bait her hook. Tonight she fished for answers.

It proved harder than luring the type with gills and at sunrise, she admitted defeat. With a stick clutched in each hand, she passed the ranger. His face was pinched. Jess said good morning anyway and dragged her body home.

The sticks barely cleared the balustrade when she tossed them. They clattered onto the heap, further reminders that time was disappearing.

Jess let herself into the cottage and inhaled disinfectant, ammonia and stale coffee; the smells of home. Soft murmurings confirmed the television was tuned to the usual breakfast show. Any second now, she'd hear the rumble of laughter. She smiled when it came and followed the sound to the first bedroom.

She knocked and pushed the door open. 'Morning, Dad.'

'That it is, Jess, darling.' He grinned a smile missing all front teeth. The edges of his eyes crinkled into wide arcs. 'Tell me about your day.' He patted the bed.

She told him what he needed to hear—all lies—just as she did most mornings.

He nodded, then announced, 'Porridge at seven. Potty at seven-thirty. Wash at eight. Turn up the volume.' He sat higher in the bed, smiled and laced his fingers over his shrivelled torso.

'Sure, Dad.' Tears pricked Jess's eyelids. She angled her body as she retrieved his partial denture, giving herself time to fix a happy face before she slid the falsies into his mouth.

The docs had all agreed on several things. Dad's recovery from the traumatic brain injury had plateaued – permanently. He needed familiarity and routine. Any changes should be avoided; something as dramatic as moving him from his home would be a death sentence.

Dad lived by his routine. Every morning, they followed a list of goals that lived in his head, despite him having lost most other functions. Shelley, who came to sit with him daily while Jess slept, said the afternoon was similar. Then evening was invariably a game show, dinner, news, toilet and his array of medications, with the side effect of knocking him out until the morning.

The experts were equally adamant that Jess had to work, because they couldn't survive on a carer's pension, and she needed her breaks, her fishing time, to keep her sane. She couldn't be the primary carer for her father if she didn't care for herself.

After second and third opinions matched this advice, Jess finally admitted that they were right. But their advice to 'just be and stay in the present' was impossible to follow. She couldn't *not* worry about the future. She stewed on it through all her waking hours, plus some of her sleeping ones, as her bleak dreams revealed.

What'll happen to Dad when I can't look after myself, let alone work or take care of him?

She predicted increased persecution by Barca's lot when they realised she was sick. They'd call the Weldons *the cripple and the retard* and terrorise them tirelessly.

Jess's hands curled into fists while she waited for the

porridge to heat. That couldn't happen. The bogan-three had done enough damage to their family, especially her dad.

She stirred the slop, glaring at it. *Trouble is, I still haven't found the magic answers for our happily-ever-after.*

Shortly after she'd helped her dad through the porridge, potty and wash part of his day, she picked up the ringing phone.

'Jess?'

In that word, she heard enormous pain, a tiny sob and recognised the centre manager. She said, 'It's horrible, isn't it?'

There was a long pause. She gathered he couldn't speak for emotion, so didn't push.

Eventually, he said, *'These cretins are our community leaders.'* His voice oozed with hopelessness. *'And the police motto is to "uphold the right", huh?'*

Jess snorted. 'The right to what? Do whatever they want?'

'I think it's supposed to be, to do whatever's right for the people in the community.'

They fell silent again. Jess didn't know what the manager was thinking; she was fixated on her father and his *accident*. She'd never be able to prove it but knew the same bogan-three who'd destroyed the centre had beaten Dad, knocked out his teeth and left him comatose to drown in his vomit. Worse still, he'd survived but suffered permanent brain damage and they'd called him the *retard* ever since. Only Barca had worn the blue uniform at the time, serving under his father who was the then-sergeant. The ultimate wickedness was that the cops, local doctor and magistrate all covered up and wrote off the incident as a self-induced, drunken accident. All of them lied. Shortly after, Barca received a promotion and within a few years, his cohorts joined him at the cop shop, and he assumed command when his father retired.

The manager cut into her thoughts. *'The insurance company's bailed.'*

'What do you mean?'

'There was no break-in. People we'd "granted access" caused the damage. So they won't pay up.'

'God, that's awful.' The same thing had happened with her dad's total and permanent disability insurance because of the lies told by their so-called community leaders.

'I'm sorry to do this to you, Jess.'

The manager sighed and Jess clenched the receiver. She anticipated what was coming.

'We'll have to put the office fit-out on hold for a week, maybe longer, until we get this mess sorted and figure out how we'll fix the place without an insurance payout.'

Jess shook her head. *No work, no income, oh, the joys of casual labour.* It wasn't his fault, but it sucked.

Her dad interrupted with, 'Jess! You're late.'

She checked her watch. He was right. She should be reading to him by now.

The rest of the day followed its usual flow. Jess slept when she usually did, though she wouldn't go into work tonight. As she'd suspected, her boss didn't have anything else for her. Until the community centre project resumed or something new came in, she was unemployed.

After tea, she gave her dad his meds and read to him until he dropped into a snuffling slumber. But with no work that night, she left the van in the garage and her overalls in the cupboard. She stayed by his bedside and watched him sleep.

Jess loved her dad so much that a vice clamped her torso until her heart felt ready to explode. But it was mostly the memory of her dad that she loved. The burly bloke he'd been up until a decade ago. He'd run his own cabinetmaking shop and was proud when his girl joined the business, renaming it Weldon & Daughter, Fine Cabinetry. They'd worked together, and in their spare time, bushwalked, fished and camped together. They'd debated world affairs and competed on every level: who could read more books, catch more fish, run faster, knock up a piece of furniture quicker… Oh, she'd had boyfriends and he'd dated a bit, but the boyfriends came second to her dad and nobody replaced her mum, who'd died when Jess was a kid.

All that changed after the accident. They lost the business. Jess's boyfriend dumped her, saying it was too hard to date a girl whose dad was her dependent. She lacked the energy for a social life, anyway. Dad only remembered the banal stuff, his daily routine rather than politics. They couldn't fish or camp any more.

And around then, the hooliganism and jobs-for-mates culture spread to infiltrate the town, deeper and darker than ever before.

In a black mood now, Jess left her dad and sat in the lounge with the lights off, anger and despair swirling in her mind. She stayed motionless for a long time.

She squinted as gaps in the curtains emitted a bright light before registering the sound of car engines. She frowned. They never had guests. Shelley, the district nurses or doctors were the only ones besides Jess to step over the threshold these days.

She cocked her head and tensed. Her gut warned her who'd pulled up their driveway and that they weren't there for a friendly visit but payback for last night.

Jess dropped to her hands and knees and crawled towards the window. She pressed her ear against the wall. The bogans were talking in low voices. They hadn't expected their cars to reveal their arrival and certainly weren't advertising it now.

She heard fragments of the conversation. '…the jerrycans…' '…time to have us a big bonfire…' Her stomach knotted as she panicked.

Though she remained quite strong, her body randomly defied her brain. The multiple sclerosis held her nervous system captive. But somehow, she had to get her dad to safety.

Jess recognised her few, slim advantages. The bogans probably thought she'd gone to work and anticipated that only her dad was at home. Plus, she had brains and stubbornness on her side. Numerous times in past years, she'd contacted the media, by phone, email and snail mail. She'd struck disbelief, sympathy and *Sorry, but we need more to excite the producer, get the budget and do a story*. But after bugging them so often, she'd worn down one of the Channel Nine reporters and Jess had his direct line saved to her mobile.

Jess sent a quick text to that number and flicked her phone onto silent. Almost instantly, she received a reply. Meanwhile, she heard the scrape of something over metal. She visualised Barca's gang lugging jerrycans off their utes.

I've gotta get Dad out of the house.

Before she went to his room, Jess clicked some functions on her mobile and carefully tucked it behind the curtain, facing it through the full-length front window. She might not capture all the sound, but live-streamed vision should do.

She felt bad doing it, but she stuffed a clean hankie into her dad's mouth as soon as she woke him. He mumbled behind the gag as she hauled him from bed. She fretted that his wasted legs barely made it to the bathroom when he was wide-awake; he now had to get to the garage, groggy with sleep and medication.

Barca called, 'We're gonna fry us some retard tonight.'

Jess's bowels cramped. Her dad must've recognised primal fear in her face and whispers because he squeezed her arm and grabbed his four-footed cane with the other hand. Jess screamed inside her head, telling her body not to let them down. *Tomorrow, you can lay me up. Tonight, you have to get us out.*

Somehow, they reached the back door. The taunts of

Barca's gang were vicious. But they still seemed to be coming from the front of the cottage. Jess shut her eyes for two seconds, praying she was right.

She slowly disengaged the lock, cringing at the loud snick. She pushed down the lever and drew the door open, inch-by-inch, sweating on whether the hinges would squeak. Fortunately, they didn't.

She and her dad were nearly running on empty. The space between the back step and garage seemed enormous. If her leg failed, they were doomed.

They navigated the step as glass splintered and the men's voices ratcheted upwards.

Her dad gripped Jess's arm so hard, his fingernails bit into her skin. She hugged and half-dragged him to the garage, expecting a fist to crack her skull.

They made it inside. Jess leaned on the van, panting. Her dad was crying; silent tears, fearful and confused. She hoped her mobile was catching it all and pictured the *breaking news* headline hitting screens of people who lived in normal places, who, if it weren't for the recording, would find it impossible to believe the depravity in her town.

Jess heard the cries inside the house grow frenzied. She figured the cops had discovered her dad's empty bed. *Now or never.* She pushed him up into the van, thankful she was used to carrying cupboards that weighed more than he did. After buckling him in, she jumped behind the wheel, pulled on her seatbelt and cranked the engine.

'Brace, Dad.'

He looked at her, eyes wild. She demonstrated. He copied. She planted her foot and aimed at the shed doors, rammed them open and drove through flying debris. The van sailed down the yard straight at the rear gate. She'd never been more grateful for living on a corner block with dual access. Then she imagined Barca and his gang following them. Her van didn't have half the guts of their tricked-up utes, but she'd try her hardest to outsmart them.

Jess calculated. The main road was close but once she hit that, they'd be sitting targets. She aimed the van down the semi-residential street and heard air horns not far behind. Jess fixed her eyes ahead and jammed her foot on the accelerator.

Lights rebounded off her rear-vision mirror into her eyes. She ducked the spheres of white and focused forward. She flat-footed the accelerator and the van's engine screamed.

More air horns, yells, brighter light from the rear. She figured they'd turned on their spotlights. Jess's van fishtailed as she turned left, overcorrected, ground the gears and just made the next right turn. The tyres skidded and scrunched on gravel. She couldn't decelerate yet.

A screech of clashing metal came with a sharp forward-thrust of the van. Her head jolted and Dad moaned. She assumed Barca's monster bull bar was crushing her bumper. But it gave her the momentum she needed and pushed her through one more gate, skewing the van in a half-circle, ploughing the rough, dry grass that was the pride and joy of the town – the footy field.

Luckily, she'd come through the gate at the opposite end to play. But an angry mob swarmed on the van from the field, stands and parked cars circling the boundary, irate at the interruption and curious.

Past her dad, through the side window, she saw Barca's lot advance. They scowled when they spotted what she'd seen in the hands of swelling numbers in the crowd – upheld mobile phones, recording the action as Jess had done back at their house.

Hodgey fisted towards her van but Simo slapped down his arm, loath to have their aggression immortalised. But Jess knew the damage had already been done – here in the past two minutes, plus back home. Her breath came out in a sob, then her face broke into a grin as she watched the men retreat.

Jess's grin broadened. Though much of the mob was still angry, she hadn't seen old friends and neighbours so animated in years. The energy they displayed had existed only in her memories, a place where the good times with her dad had been relegated. She watched the townsfolks' passion fire, knowing there wouldn't be a happily-ever-after for the cripple and the retard, but maybe this was a silver lining.

GUN OIL, BACON AND BLEACH

Winner Scarlet Stiletto Awards 2017
Special Commendation

GUN OIL, BACON AND BLEACH

Ash lathered her hands with sanitiser, grimacing because despite the antiseptic scent and the soothing action, the reek of murder clung on. An illusion, as was the insect crawl tickling her skin, and neither would stop her doing her job. But it drove her crazy that she couldn't break the chronic habit.

This time, it'd been sparked by an image on her computer screen: a black steel fence swathed in flowers and pictures. Her eyes returned to a collage of names and love hearts that surrounded a naïve drawing of a female with blonde curls. And as before, her gaze locked on the five words in the centre, scrawled in a rainbow of coloured crayon: 'We MISS YOU Miss Binchey.'

A voice came from behind, startling Ash. 'Fourth day in a row.'

She twisted around as the librarian added, 'We'll have to charge you rent, at this rate,' then laughed at her own joke. 'What're you up to, cuz?'

Ash minimised the internet browser as Fin went to crane over her shoulder and said, 'Research.'

'Well, duh.' Fin smirked. 'We all know the famous AR Clarke is writing another bestseller.'

Ash cringed at her older cousin's blatant fishing for details and changed the subject. 'I'm staying at Mum's –'

'Run from your bloke, did you?'

Her cousin leaned in and pushed at the fading bruise on Ash's cheek, drawing a sharp wince. She stopped her answering retort by focusing on the heavy pucker lines around Fin's mouth; signs of her acerbic wit as much as middle-age.

'Funny, isn't it? No way in hell you'd have come back to Picadunyah otherwise – that's what Mum reckons.'

Ash tensed. She had last seen her aunt when she was five years old, and never forgotten her open hostility. Apparently, that hadn't changed.

Fin talked on. 'Heard a tree did a job on your mum's house. How're the repairs going?'

Relieved to be on safer turf, Ash said, 'Why do you think I'm camped here at the library?' She shook her head. 'No power, meaning no modem, no internet, and no computer after my battery goes flat, and me, Mum and the tradies getting in each other's way. Best I stay clear during the day or I won't survive writing this book.'

Fin's face got busy, she was obviously working up to saying something and Ash sensed the hard question was coming.

She scrambled for a diversion, going with, 'Can you point me to a good reference on shotguns?' She didn't need it as she'd accumulated plenty, including a direct line to a firearms expert in the police force, but the ruse worked.

Her cousin scratched at her chin. 'Textbook, 'net or person?'

Ash hadn't expected that answer and tipped her head. In her experience, things from left-field could be gifts of gold as often as they bombed. 'Person.'

'Bernie Chandler had the gun shop on Main Street.' Fin waved, saying, 'You wouldn't remember,' which sounded critical. 'Been retired for years, but still knows more about guns than anyone 'round here.'

'Where would I find him?'

Fin gave her a look that said Ash didn't belong in the town she'd been born in twenty-nine years ago. 'The pub.'

Ash stepped into the room, stirring dust motes in light that shafted through the windows. Her skin itched, as several pairs of eyes raked over her and before she had the chance to ask for Bernie Chandler, the bartender thumbed to a humpbacked old man with leathery skin propping up the bar.

When she introduced herself, Chandler sucked his front teeth, then muttered, 'We knows who ya're.'

Not a promising start, but her 'Get you a beer?' earned a semi-smile.

It still took four pots and a bag of chips for him to loosen up, then a counter meal of bangers and mash before she figured he was primed. By then, she'd mentally rephrased her question for the hundredth time, aiming for an offhand way to ask about the weapon used by Brian McKelvey to kill Louisa Binchey and two of his earlier victims.

'Did you see many Browning 12-gauge shotguns through your shop?'

The old man laughed. It turned into a wheeze, settling after he slapped his leg.

'Ya're a city slicker, ain't ya?'

Not by choice, but she curbed her response.

'The Browning shotty was as common as muck 'round here back then.' Chandler leaned forward, rattling out another chuckle. 'Half the farms had 'em.' He added, 'Geez, I 'member selling one to your dad and your granddad.'

Apart from diverting her cousin from the sticky question about her book and adding to her understanding of McKelvey's shotgun of choice, her chat with Chandler was three hours and forty-odd bucks wasted. Ash decided to work off her frustration. Or until her laptop went flat.

While navigating the internet, she listened to her mum chattering to the dogs outside. Hearing her mum happy was worth returning for and so was finishing this book, but she'd go back to the city after delivering the manuscript. She scratched her skin as her mind split between wondering how she could keep Ren out of her life once she went back, and what she'd pulled up on her computer.

Police have called for a social media blackout following the arrest of a man for the alleged abduction and murder of schoolteacher Louisa Binchey, 26.

How different it'd been for Louisa than McKelvey's earlier victims. Two didn't even rate national news until he'd fronted the committal hearing for killing Louisa, while her murder evoked an outpouring of grief that almost jeopardised McKelvey's prosecution. But as much as the syndrome of sympathy for attractive, white, well-off female victims irked Ash, and as much as it went against her credo that all victims should be treated equally, she knew if it weren't for Louisa, the cold cases would've remained unsolved.

A warning flashed on Ash's screen: *Battery less than 7%*. She shut down the computer and sat in her oil lamp-lit childhood bedroom with book research eddying in her mind.

She lifted her fingers to her nose and inhaled the metallic scent of blood, but something else too. For some reason, she fancied it was oil, but not for cooking, squeaky hinges or cars. This was almost tactile, and it was probably only her shotgun research that made her mind jump to gun oil.

Ash couldn't concentrate the next morning. For hours, she was alone in the library with Fin and her cousin's assistant. For the most, few words were exchanged; little beyond the infrequent customer or hum of lights and computers to break the silence. Maybe that was her problem; it was too quiet compared to her usual haunts in Brunswick. She flicked her gaze to the four women's images on her laptop and immediately doubted it.

She supposed her restlessness could stem from being at that pivotal moment where, with the background covered, she commenced key interviews and the human factor came to the fore. *Truth is stranger than fiction* was never more spot-on than for a true-crime writer. Any of these interviews could take her unaware and send the book into a serious cant, complicating her objectivity or necessitating a fresh look at everything.

Ash shrugged, unsure if that was her problem today either. Distracted by her odd mood, she grabbed her mobile phone when it rang, checking the screen automatically. *Ren.* She rejected his call and waited for the inevitable beep. He'd averaged three messages a day since she'd left. She deleted the latest unheard.

With the mobile still in her hand, Ash ran her eyes over the library. The assistant had gone on an errand. Her cousin was in conversation with another woman and her body language indicated it'd be a long chat. The place was otherwise deserted. She might as well set the ball rolling.

Ash dialled the number for McKelvey's defacto, revelling in the rise of adrenaline as she listened to the rings. Then Tania Brodie's voicemail switched on, the beep went, and she found herself saying, 'This is Ashley Clarke,' followed by her form blurb.

Next, she phoned Barwon Prison, confirming she was on McKelvey's visitor list and her appointment for the following week. She ticked that off, and started to key in a fresh number.

'You're writing about Louisa Binchey?'

Ash's pulse thumped. The truth couldn't be avoided forever. She swivelled around admitting, 'Yeah.' She and Fin held a long look. 'All of Brian McKelvey's victims, actually.'

Her cousin's pupils contracted to pinpricks on her pale blue eyes. Guilt knotted in Ash's stomach. She wasn't writing about this for fame or fortune or to hurt other people, Fin included. Since she was a small girl—long before Louisa Binchey's death—Ash knew she had to write about McKelvey. It was her purpose in life. But she'd had to cut her teeth on two other books before she could tell this story.

Fin shook her head. 'How could you?' Without waiting for an answer, she pivoted and stalked outside, drawing her mobile from her pocket.

The afternoon felt endless, stretching Ash's nerves. Fin hadn't spoken to her again and Ash pretended to be oblivious to her evil-eye glare. She had stood up to Ren's abuse; she could cope with her country cousin.

She shuffled her index cards, again questioning the cause of her agitation today. The ping on her mobile only vaguely registered, but she snapped alert after thumbing open a new message.

'GET A LIFE!' Written in all caps, unsigned and from someone outside her contact list.

Ash located Fin, who seemed to be busy emptying a crate of returns, and watched her cousin as she dialled the sender's number: no reaction and the call rang out.

She chewed over other possibilities. McKelvey's defacto might be trying to scare her off. Her eyebrows lifted, thinking Ren could be getting more creative, hoping to drive her back to Melbourne with veiled threats, since begging hadn't worked. Or perhaps McKelvey had changed his tune. He'd apparently enjoyed the media attention during his trial, and he'd jumped at her request for an interview, but he might be playing her, making her work harder for it.

Ash thought about blocking the number, but didn't, curious rather than intimidated. Then she again fixed on the four images on her computer, and the niggle in her gut increased.

She sat forward on the sweaty, hard plastic seat, muttering, 'I still don't get it.'

The women fell into an age-span of twenty-three through to Ash's age: twenty-nine. Each was single, blonde and white, though only Louisa and Rachel were stunning, which possibly accounted for why Kristen and Jodie had drawn little press, as unjust as that was.

The police had found McKelvey's gun, bearing his clear fingerprints. And though unable to retrieve the gun's serial number, forensics matched the round in the chamber to the shell casings found at the killing scenes of Louisa, Kristen and Rachel.

All the crimes linked to Picadunyah, this little town in the sticks with a population of ninety-seven, its greatest claim to fame a bark hut pub allegedly frequented by the Kelly Gang back in the bushranger days. Rachel was killed five kilometres up the road from the library. The other three were abducted from different parts of Melbourne and brought to the bush on Picadunyah's outskirts.

It all fitted, forensically and, on the whole, logistically. But the differences had always bugged Ash. She ran through them again.

The crimes against Louisa, Kristen and Jodie had occurred over seven years and within this decade, while Rachel was killed in 1993.

McKelvey had abducted and held Louisa for two weeks. He'd repeatedly assaulted her, then killed her from behind, buckshot raining her body, piercing her heart and other major organs. Kristen's fate eighteen months' prior had been almost identical, except she'd died six days after McKelvey snatched her. Before that, Jodie had been treated similarly, aside from McKelvey letting her go after two nights.

On the other hand, Rachel hadn't been abducted or assaulted, but killed at home, on the farm she'd shared with her widowed mother, sister and now-deceased grandparents. She'd been shot front-on, in the face.

The mass of evidence appeared irrefutable and the court had convicted McKelvey of all three murders, and Jodie's abduction and assault. Yet, despite remaining silent on three cases during the investigation and trials, McKelvey had often protested his innocence for one: Rachel. But what bothered Ash most was that offenders were known to escalate from assault to murder. Not the other way around.

She whispered, 'Rachel and Jodie are in the wrong order.'

Ash's hatchback kicked up a cloud of dust as she turned into her mum's driveway. Not for the first time, she saw the irony in that she'd spent her first five years here, but it would never be her home. She pulled up behind the house and spotted the dogs confined to their pen. Odd. And so was the absence of tradies' utes in the yard.

With one foot inside the house, she was unnerved by its silence and gloom. Since she'd been here, the curtains had been pulled wide for natural light during the days; oil lamps and candles casting a warm glow at night. Today, the windows were covered.

'Mum?'

No answer.

Dread weighed on Ash and she called out again. Something from the distant past or perhaps purely innate dragged her feet to the main bedroom. She pushed open the door and saw her mum lying on the bed, tucked into herself.

'You okay?'

Unable to understand the muffled reply, she edged into the room and lit the lamp by the bed. At Ash's tentative touch to her shoulder, her mum turned. Her face was puffy and blotchy in the flickering light.

'Why, Ashie?' A nasal twang from crying.

So, word's already gotten around.

'Someone has to tell Rachel's story.' Ash reached for her mum's hand. 'Someone that can be objective, but who cares.'

Her mum sighed, the sound long and quivery.

'I was going to tell you…' Ash didn't finish. Her reasons seemed weak now.

'You'll do it well.' Her mum curled her fingers around Ash's. 'Your dad used to send me all your stories, along with your school reports, so I could see how great you were turning out. I've read your books three times.' She gave another sigh. 'So proud of you. Probably forgot to tell you that.' A tear leaked and rolled into the side of her mouth.

She *had* forgotten. Ash brushed away the wet trail on her mum's cheek.

'I'm sorry I wasn't a good mum, Ashie.'

'Shush. Don't say that.'

'What sort of woman tells her husband to leave and take her baby?' Exhaustion layered into her words. 'You two were the best parts of my life. And now he's gone. And you're all grown up.'

Their fingers squeezed together.

'But Ashie…this story…it's black.'

She slipped out of Ash's clasp and coiled into a ball.

'Fin wants to know if you'll be working here much longer.' The library assistant wouldn't meet Ash's gaze. 'Says it's bad for business.'

'Really?' Ash's eyes swept the building. She'd never seen a crowd in Picadunyah to rival this one. She stared at the back of Fin's blonde-and-grey streaked head and added, 'Tell her I'll be here a while yet.'

The girl nodded and joined a huddled group. They whispered among themselves, shooting her glances.

Ash's mobile gave a timely vibration. Her caller wasn't in her contacts, which included the new one she'd added yesterday as *Anon SMS*.

'Hello?'

She heard the clang of a tram and the wisp of breathing down the line.

Then, *'Why're you doing this?'*

'Ren?'

'You belong here, Ash,' he whined. *'With me.'*

'Not true.'

'Give me another chance. Please!'

She thought about their good times. Then the toxic ones. 'No, Ren. I told you: once might've been an accident, but hit me twice and I'm gone.'

Silence hung before he asked, *'You close to wrapping up the McKelvey story?'*

'It's coming along.' Ash instantly regretted letting him engage her.

'Still writing in the library?' When she didn't answer, he added, *'Come home. You'll get it done quicker here.'*

'It's not my home anymore.' She pictured his face and urged, 'Ren, let me go. We both need to move on.'

'Get back here.' There was quiet fury in his tone.

'No.' Ash steeled herself. 'And don't call me again…on your own phone or any other. It's stalking, it's an offence and I'll report you to the police. Got it?'

'Ash –'

Her hand shook as she disconnected, but she pulsed with energy. Then she picked up a new SMS, noting the sender was her anonymous communicator.

'GO HOME OR YOU'LL BE NEWS YOURSELF WHEN THEY FIND YOUR BODY IN THE LIBRARY.'

The cop eyed her. 'And you think this is the work of your boyfriend?'

'*Ex*-boyfriend,' Ash corrected.

'Not sure myself if this is anything but him being a bit overenthusiastic.' His ocker drawl gave the word extra syllables.

'It's a threat.'

Sergeant Bateman regarded her, eventually saying, 'You could as easily see it as a warning to take care – him showing concern that your book is going to get you into strife.'

Ash thought about emails or texts she'd sent in the past that recipients had misunderstood because tone was difficult to convey electronically. 'I suppose.'

'Glad you agree.' Bateman gave a string of nods, then a broad smile. 'And this,' he nudged her phone, 'could've easily come from someone other than your boyfriend, couldn't it?'

He had her there, too.

'But the timing –'

'Could be coincidental.' He paused, before adding, 'Now, say for a moment that it is a threat, what you're writing about's stirred up things around here, so plenty'd have a bigger stake than your boyfriend in stopping you. Agreed?'

He made sense. Between allies and loved ones of McKelvey and his four victims, a host of people held high emotion about the cases. Some still believed he'd been wrongly convicted. Others were desperate for answers. Ash deflated.

The sergeant flapped the blank form. 'So, do you still want to go ahead with reporting your boyfriend as a stalker?'

When Ash arrived at her mum's place that afternoon, she found the tradies packing up, but no sign of her mum or the dogs.

She took the chance to wander into the lounge room, which was unaffected by the fallen tree, but rarely used in favour of the nook adjacent to the kitchen. Standing in the middle, she revolved slowly, and her eyes flicked over the walls and shelves, couch and scattered floor rugs. The deep chuckles of her dad, and her mum singing and strumming a guitar, were as real as what she could see. This room had barely changed in the intervening years, if her pre-schooler memory was reliable.

Slightly giddy when she stopped spinning, Ash drifted to a shelf of photographs and knickknacks, her throat tightening when she saw souvenirs that must've been sent by her dad, along with a few from her mum's rare, brittle visits with them in Thornbury.

For a few minutes, she tried to visualise what her life would've been like if she and Dad had stayed in Picadunyah.

She couldn't.

Ash swung her legs from the car the next morning and eyed the farmhouse. *Still white with a red-painted tin roof.* She couldn't make out the figure on the porch until she reached the bottom step.

'So, you've come then.' Despite yet another day breaking sultry, the woman wrapped her arms around herself as if chilled. 'Expected it, since Fin told me what you're up to.'

She tipped her head towards the door, leading the way inside and through to the kitchen.

'Sit. I'll get us some lemonade.'

Ash nodded, surprised by the crush on her chest as she watched Aunt Kerry pull a jug from the fridge, extract two glasses from the dresser and pour. The scene was somehow as familiar as the cladding outside.

Kerry sat directly in front of Ash. Her expression kept changing and was impossible to gauge. 'Been a long time.'

'It has.' Ash took a swallow of lemonade. Flavour filled her mouth and she blurted out, 'Nan's recipe?'

'Yep.'

'It's good.'

Kerry nodded and they lapsed into silence.

Ash skimmed over the room, assessing it was as unchanged as her mum's lounge, then felt intrusive and dropped her eyes. A second later, she flinched when Kerry's fingers stroked her jawline, angling her face towards the light. Luckily, the bruise from Ren had healed.

'Knew you'd be a stunner…just like my Rach.'

Ash had remembered this house and Kerry as unfriendly, at odds now with her aunt's soft touch and a stream of other memories. Happy ones. Of the table between them crammed with food. Her cousins, Fin and Rachel—one plain, the other gorgeous, but both so grown-up—bickering playfully. Her aunt shucking under Ash's chin. Ash's mum and Kerry throwing their arms around each other. Her mum and dad boot-scooting in front of the stove, and being told to *Take it outside* by her laughing nan, while Pa turned the page of his newspaper, giving it a shake.

Ash's breath caught and she met Kerry's moist eyes. Her aunt roughly swiped away a tear and retrieved a framed picture from the windowsill.

'You're the spitting image of her. Now I know what she would've looked like at your age, if she hadn't been taken from me.'

Ash studied the photo, seeing Rachel with fresh eyes. She wore her own hair shorter and wasn't anywhere near as pretty as her cousin, but they could've passed for sisters.

Ash travelled along the main street and shifted in her car seat, wrinkling her nose at sweat gliding towards her butt. *And it's only 9.00am.* She traded thoughts from another imminent scorcher to her priorities.

Unless Tania Brodie was her anonymous anti-penfriend, she hadn't responded to Ash's call, so a follow-up was high on the list, along with contacting McKelvey's mother. Both could wait a little, though.

Likewise, she'd sit on the SMS sent to her phone last night. 'STAY OUT OF IT.' A threat, not a warning, with its appended, 'OR YOU DIE NEXT!' Without fresh leads on her stalker, the police couldn't act.

She decided to focus on Aunt Kerry for now. But then her mind skittered to a blogger's words she'd read before bed last night.

With no links between McKelvey and Rachel Alistair except shell casings and semen residue, did the cops and courts get it wrong?

Fatigued already thanks to her overactive mind, Ash yawned. In the next instant, she passed Fin, who was turning from the opposite direction into the library car park. She answered her cousin's glare with a small wave and drove on.

Minutes later, Kerry met her on the porch as she had yesterday, except this time she was wearing a tenuous smile.

'Want to see through the rest of the place first?'

'Please.'

Ash followed her aunt inside and into the first room off the hallway. She scanned, taking in that again, little had changed. Her eyes fell on a large mirror that pulled her in to stroke its carved frame, then press a flower on the corner. After a click, she slid the mirror sideways, revealing an empty rack.

'Got rid of 'em.' Kerry cleared her throat. 'Couldn't bear having guns in the place after Rach –' She broke off.

Ash nodded, while her mind strayed.

No gun found at the scene, no witnesses, no motive, no leads.

Rachel's death had been relegated to cold case status until the police arrested McKelvey for Louisa's murder and subsequently linked the deaths via retrospective forensic tests.

She glanced at a faded spot on the couch and recalled from the case file that McKelvey's semen had been found there. *Yet Rachel wasn't raped and he'd used condoms for the others?*

Her thoughts flitted to her conversation with old Bernie

Chandler and she met Kerry's gaze in the mirror. 'Did McKelvey use Pa's Browning?'

Kerry rubbed at furrows crisscrossing her forehead. 'It went missing that day. I never told anyone.' She waved limply to the gun closet. 'I couldn't face that I was to blame. That storing the guns in that thing instead of a proper locked safe handed him the weapon to kill my Rach.'

Ash felt conflicted. Her aunt was a virtual stranger, and as a widow and farmer she had to be strong. She might rebuff consolation from her niece or crave it.

Kerry sniffed and saved Ash with, 'Ready to see more?'

She nodded. Trailing behind Kerry, she vaguely thought she heard something outside. *Was that a car?* Then she remembered the message she was to pass on.

'Mum's finding this hard, too.'

Understatement.

Kerry stopped with her back to Ash.

'She wrote to you, but kept it, never sent it. I didn't know until she made me read this.' Ash pulled a note from her pocket. 'Mum can't forgive herself because Rachel rang her that day…something wasn't right, but she waited until after my nap to come over. It was too late.'

Kerry turned slowly and took the paper. Her lips silently mouthed the words as she read the note, then pursed. 'I sensed something was wrong, too, but stayed at the sales yard instead of coming home.' She did a hard swallow. 'I haven't forgiven myself for that and the gun safe yet, but I'm living with it.' She refolded the paper. 'So, you tell your mum, twenty-four years is too long to punish herself sick and to be without her big sister.'

They exchanged a sad glance and Kerry walked on, showing Ash through each room. They paused at the threshold of the last bedroom.

'The girls' room?'

Her aunt nodded. 'You can look around. I'd prefer not to.'

She pointed. 'Fin lives in town now, but best not disturb her side.'

Ash appreciated being left to explore. She found a folder of short stories and realised that on top of their physical resemblance, she shared a love of writing with her dead cousin. While she flicked through Rachel's photo albums, her skin tingled.

After exhausting what remained of Rachel's life, she spotted more albums on Fin's shelf and figured a peek wouldn't hurt. Flicking through, Ash noted that many of the family photographs were duplicates of Rachel's, but while her dead cousin had also been captured in social and academic settings, Fin's collection only revealed that she liked wildlife.

Ash flipped a page and several polaroid photos scattered. She swooped to rescue them, her eyes widening as she picked them up. These deviated from Fin's pet subjects and were of a motorbike, a campfire, and the bush out of town. Another pictured only two pairs of tightly entwined jeaned legs. The next made her gasp, then peer closer. In a clumsy selfie, Fin smiled at the camera and clung to McKelvey, whose lips hovered over a fresh love bite on her breast.

Ash's hands turned slick with sweat and she wiped them on her legs. Thoughts tussled for attention. Unlike McKelvey's other three victims, Rachel hadn't been abducted or sexually assaulted, and she was shot in the face, not from behind, with Pa's Browning.

She lurched to her feet, assailed by the smells of flesh, gun oil, bacon and bleach, and dizzy with a flashback to her mum screaming, *Ashie, go inside! Now!* Mum had pushed her towards the kitchen, blocking something: Rachel's body.

Her adult-self ran to the kitchen, but her perspective warped to seeing it as her preschool version. Scarily real, she smelt congealed bacon fat on a plate, saw a dirty rag and small oil bottle, and watched Fin come in, pulling down the shoulder of her top and massaging a large red welt. Then Fin noticed Ash and bore down on her, propelling her into the wall. With arms either side of Ash's head, Fin's skin reeked of bleach and her face screwed in anger.

The scene blurred into a jumble of memories—people in tears or shouting, sirens howling, her mum crying and locking herself in her room—all stowed away by her five-year-old mind. Until now.

Ash jolted from the past when fingers bit into the skin on her forearm.

'You know, don't you, cuz?'

She met Fin's eyes. They were filled with the same venom she'd seen the day Rachel died. It struck her that the welt on Fin's shoulder must have been a wound from shotgun recoil, and she'd used bleach in scrubbing off her sister's blood. It also made sense of the threats Ash had received. Fin didn't want her writing the book.

Ash backed towards the dresser. 'You killed her.'

'Well, duh.'

She thought about her beautiful dead cousin, the polaroid selfie of Fin all over McKelvey and his semen on the couch. 'You were McKelvey's girlfriend, but he fancied Rachel and you couldn't handle that.'

Fin's eyes narrowed. 'Smart.' She laughed. 'But not smart enough.' She loomed at Ash.

But Ash side-stepped, and when she yanked open the dresser drawer, her fingertips touched Nan's rolling pin, where it had always belonged. Then it was in her palm, feeling solid and heavy, as her cousin clamped her hands around Ash's neck. Wheezing, and with her eyes filling with spots, Ash swung the timber into the side of Fin's head. But the blow didn't stop her. Fin gripped harder. Ash couldn't hold the handle anymore. Her vision swam.

She heard a grunt, then the pressure on her neck released. She staggered back and watched Fin crumple.

'I wouldn't have believed it, if I hadn't heard her myself.'

Ash wheeled to her aunt, who dropped the rolling pin marbled with her daughter's blood.

'But somehow, it doesn't surprise me. Does that mean I'm not a good mum?'

It echoed what Ash's mum had said. But in truth, all their troubles were due to Fin and her love of a bad man. Ash shook her head.

Kerry exhaled, long and slow. 'I'll call Sergeant Bateman.'

DUPLICITY

Winner Scarlet Stiletto Awards 2018
Special Commendation

DUPLICITY

I watch the pulse in your neck. Tick. Tick. Tick. Nothing. A pause so long that I hold my breath. This can't be it; we need more time. We'd planned to learn French and Skype a nice couple that we'd alternately holiday with in France and Australia, stomp grapes and quaff wine, tan ourselves golden on as many nudist beaches as we could notch up. Haven't done it yet.

You still haven't breathed. My heart is in my throat – I understand that saying now. I am about to call for a nurse when you take a deep, shuddering breath. And two more. You sigh, and your exhalation brushes my skin.

Looking into your eyes, I stroke your forehead and see that you are still in there. Still with me. My lips make weak upwards curves, and somehow my taut vocal cords manage, 'I love you, Guy.'

Your mouth pulls at the corners as you try to smile back.

Some days I sit with you and I have nothing to say. I feel guilty, overthinking the things I could talk about, how our mostly one-sided conversation could go. Me chattering about things you can't enjoy or care about. I've taken long service leave and am here every day. What does it matter to you if it's Wednesday or Friday? And why torment you with how gorgeous it is outside—cool but clear, the breeze scented with blossom—while you lie in your bed?

Other days, the silence in your room—barring the rhythmic hiss of air releasing from or filling your air mattress, and the rattle within the air-conditioning system—tortures me, and I can't still my tongue. There is no filter between my thoughts and what comes out of my mouth.

Today is a bit of both. I'm not sure I should share what's on my mind but feel driven to. I shift to the window and spy movement in the courtyard garden.

'There's a willy wagtail out there, Guy.'

The tiny bird darts around, its fantail twitching.

'Your mum used to say willy wagtails are the bringer of bad news, remember? Fascinated by Aboriginal folklore, wasn't she? I've heard another version of the *jitta jitta* legend – they bring spirit children to their mothers.'

With that opening, I turn and look at you. 'Do you know what today is?'

Your eyes are open, but you could be asleep. Nothing changes on your face, not even when I say, 'Her birthday.'

I work hard to keep my voice even. Seated again, I hold your hand and talk about our Meaghan. Memories of long ago. Thoughts of what might have been.

'She'd have been thirty today, same age as me when we had her. Maybe she would've had her own baby by now. Imagine us as grandparents.'

I sense something and focus on you. You're staring at the ceiling, unblinking, face immobile. But your eyes are glazed. A tear slides down your cheek that I capture with a tissue.

You're still in there. Still with me.

Back at home later, I shut myself in your study and light a fire. It pops and crackles, but I have to chafe my arms for warmth as I'm pacing the floorboards. Unsettled. Lonely.

For over a decade, our routine has been patterned. We'd have lasagne, garlic bread, trifle and a lamington sponge—all Meaghan's favourites—to mark what was her birthday. Overfull on overly rich foods, we'd come in here, put on the fire, go through the family photos and wonder how our girl would have changed as she grew into a woman. Brood over why she had to die just shy of sixteen.

I look at the albums and keepsakes. Do the wondering, the brooding alone, ridiculously put out that you've left all of this to me. Sitting at your desk, I guess it is mine now. Or it will be soon. Too soon. With that sad truth and Meaghan on my mind, I don't want to go to bed until my eyes are blurred and grainy with fatigue. Maybe then I'll sleep through without waking suddenly, crying out, face wet with tears.

It has all happened so fast. You went into hospital for an overnight stay, a bunch of scans and tests, and within a week were transferred to the hospice, rapidly deteriorating. No time to plan, set things in place. There might already be actions needing attention, accounts overdue, so I start to go through your drawers.

There is a folder with a small number of bills, one due this week, but that can't be everything. Which bills are paid automatically from our bank, or come through on your email?

I am out of touch. Have been since Meaghan's body was retrieved from Red Point, her bike abandoned on the cliff above, leaning on the bench where she loved to watch the waves, think, dream. She wouldn't have jumped – everyone agreed on that. An accident, they said, she slipped somehow. But my grief and fear and doubt grew until you took me to Emergency, where we were ushered through for psych assessment, and whatever last strands that bound me broke. Sobbing, I slithered to the floor and you hugged me tightly for a long time. I remember that clearly, even though my recovery is mostly a blur. The person who came out the other side is not the same Darcy Moordish. I'm still dedicated to my job—Senior Flavourist at AVA Essences—but useless at the mundane: shopping, housework, bill paying, which landed on you. And I've learnt to keep my doubts about our Meaghan's death to myself.

I am ashamed at my morbid mood. I search for happy memories of the three of us to honour Meaghan's birthday. It works until I come across a sheet of loose-leaf lined paper, creased from folding and unfolding. The handwriting rings of the past.

Reading it aloud, my voice quivers. '"I can't do this anymore."'

Searching back, I can't place the writing but know I should be able to, and those five words on the A4 page touch me. The note must've been important for you to keep it.

I fall asleep at your desk, thinking the gap in our lives has grown wider than I'd realised.

All intention of asking you about the note is forgotten when I go into the hospice the next morning. You had a bad night. Restless, in pain, vomiting. The ward nurse has given you extra meds and, holding your hand, I ask, 'Are you in pain now?'

'No.' A hoarse whisper.

We sit awhile silently. The air-conditioner is extra rattly today. You manage to lift a hand and wave towards your mouth.

'Do you want some ice?'

You make an O with your finger and thumb, meaning yes, and I bring some from the dispenser and slip it between your dry lips from a teaspoon, reminding me of feeding Meaghan as a baby. Life does a circle.

After a few spoonfuls, you let out an exhausted sigh and signal you are done. You stare my way. There is a long gap between breaths, and I wait, counting the beats. I hate to see you suffering…the skin shrinking over your facial bones more with every day.

It seems odd that you are still tanned, have muscle tone in your arms, and those beautiful straight teeth are white. But three weeks ago, you were the top striker in your hockey team, competing, running, cycling and lifting weights with no inkling your melanoma had metastasised to your brain and lungs. This weekend, the Panthers will play in the semi-finals without you.

I slip my hand back inside your larger one. My thumb is wrapped over yours, gently caressing your skin. I can't say the words but hope you can read my gaze.

I love you. I will be lost without you. But go now if you're ready. Don't stay for me.

A spare pillow sits at the end of your bed. I'm tempted to press it over your face and bring on your release but can't follow through. I am startled when you squeeze my fingers, grip stronger than I'd expect from a dying man. I think you have understood my message, maybe also my impulse to assist your passing, but you want a little longer, too.

I have forgotten the note and don't think of it until I'm home again that evening.

'What does it mean, Guy?'

My voice is loud in the empty house. The note bothers me. The missing bits in our life, the chasm between us and my awareness of what the last fourteen years have been like for you bothers me. I continue looking through your study, feeling like an intruder.

Going over your bookshelves, I reach a group of novels that were Meaghan's school books. I hadn't realised you'd kept them. She'd highlighted some text, scrawled comments in the margin. I read them now, hearing her voice, smiling. I've forgotten to eat but that's not uncommon these days. It is late – hours have disappeared as I've slipped into Meaghan's old world. My body is aching for bed, but one novel remains.

It opens on a folded sheet about midway. Same handwriting as the other note.

Reading it aloud, I laugh. '"Nerd. You need a life, Megs."' It's signed with a large, flowery love heart around the writer's name. I shake my head saying, 'Typical Steph.'

The girls had been best friends forever, same as me and Ebony, Stephanie's mum. A pain in my chest reminds me all that is in the past.

It was so hard to see Ebony or Stephanie after we lost Meaghan. I found words of comfort when Stephanie overdosed a year later, masking the wrongful, hurtful sense of injustice. If Stephanie was going to take her own life, why couldn't God have traded their places – left Meaghan safe and sent her friend to the bottom of the cliff?

I have tortured myself since. Did Ebony push me away because she'd guessed my selfish thoughts? But I know the wedge between us surfaced before Stephanie died – so was it that Ebony couldn't cope with my grief?

You kept me away, Guy. *For your sake*, you said, to stop me having another breakdown. I trusted you were right. But I really should call her and try again.

A new thought strikes. Stephanie wrote those words *I can't do this anymore* on a piece of paper you kept in your desk drawer. She didn't leave a suicide note. Or did she? If this is her final message, why do you have it? Why not her parents, Ebony and Logan?

The gnawing in my gut could be hunger. Or it could be a warning sign that grief and fear and doubt are all combining again, and I'm losing grip. You have constantly warned me that my mental health is an ever-fragile thing. This time I'm without you to help me retreat, arrange a stronger dose of happy pills, make apologies on my behalf. It scares me so much I give up the idea of going to bed and feverishly paw through your study.

The problem is not knowing what I'm looking for.

All night, I search for anything else that doesn't sit right. I think about your laptop. It's in the cupboard at the hospice with your bag of personal things: clothes you wore into hospital, wallet, coins, watch, keys, pyjamas, spare clothes you expected to wear coming home. You can't use the computer now.

I need to see what's on it, and go in earlier than usual.

'He had a better night,' the nurse tells me. She has kind eyes. 'I just gave him some ice cream.'

You are living off bites of ice cream, mouthfuls of sweetened tea, sips of lemonade, slivers of ice. How long can the body last like that? I don't like to ask, but the nurse seems to understand what I'm thinking.

'He could be with us for weeks yet.' Her pat to my hand is warm. She watches me make my way to your room.

Your eyes follow me as I come to your bedside. Your gaze is sometimes vacant, doped up on pain relief. Other times—like today—it searches my face for something. I'm not sure what. Maybe to remember what life used to be like? Wanting reassurances that I can't give – that your end will be a peaceful and painless slipping away into a better after-life? Asking why the doctors don't have a magic cure?

I want you to fall asleep so I can access your computer. I think about taking the laptop into your ensuite and cranking it up, but you'd recognise its start-up sound. While one of the nurses is topping up your morphine pump, I quickly extract the laptop and leave it by the door, covered with my coat. I imagine reproach in your eyes when I return to your side.

It doesn't stop me taking the computer home or turning it on, though.

It's password-protected but *darcy&meaghan* lets me in. Your email app uploads a huge number of new messages. A few personal ones from people I haven't let know about your condition. Several bills.

Dealing with that takes priority, and then I skim over your

mailbox folders. They don't reveal anything remarkable. Nothing named *Stephanie*, for instance.

I'm unhinging, I know. Why have I read so much into a note from our daughter's best friend? You might have found it in one of Meaghan's books and shoved it in your desk without thought, maybe without even looking at it. Maybe I'm on this quest so I don't have to face losing you.

It is what it is, I decide. I eventually go through the rest of your new mail and jump to conclusions about why you emptied your *Deleted* folder before you went into hospital, even though we both expected you to come home.

Suddenly, the house is suffocating and something long overdue is urgent. I'm on autopilot as I drive several streets away. I'm at the front door without recalling turning off the car, leaving it, locking it.

Logan answers. 'It's late, Darcy.'

I get the sense he means *It's too late*.

'I need to see her.'

He promises nothing and re-enters the house, pulling the door. It locks. There are raised voices and a hush before footsteps approach.

Ebony opens the door. She doesn't invite me in.

No words seem enough, but I try. 'I'm sorry I haven't been a good friend.'

An odd look crosses her face. She shrugs.

'Can we talk? Properly, I mean? Inside? Or something?' I feel wrong-footed despite being the one to make the first move.

Her gaze is sad, but there is more. A wariness? What have we done to our friendship?

She says, 'Probably best if we don't.'

'Why?'

She shakes her head and goes to shut the door.

I block it, vaguely registering pain as it hits my forearm. 'I don't understand.'

'You chose.'

'What do you mean? I don't –'

'Ask Guy.' Ebony's face is red, her neck blotchy.

'I can't.' The words choke. 'He's dying. Cancer.'

She says flatly, 'More death.'

I'm shocked and don't react when she pushes my arm away and slams the door. In a brain fog, I somehow function enough to drive back to the hospice. I don't exchange words with the ward nurse and go straight through to your room.

'What does she mean, Guy?' I ask you, after blurting out Ebony's cutting words.

Your feet wriggle under the blanket. Unfairly, it crosses my mind that it's a convenient time for your voice and hand gestures not to work. You can avoid explanations. You hate conflict. Guilt rushes over me and I feel nauseous. We have little time left – weeks, days, hours or minutes, who knows? We should be making the most of it.

'I'm sorry, Guy.'

Your forehead smooths. I lay my head on the siderail of your bed. The air mattress sighs out. I look into your eyes, hoping you see my love and believe I've let it go.

I try.

I sit with you for another two hours, chatting softly, and don't go near your study when I return home. I sort through the living room, knowing this shared zone holds only the ordinary detritus of an empty-nest couple.

My best intentions last for that night and into the next day, but as I sit with you in the afternoon, my mind worries at Stephanie's note and Ebony's rejection. I can think of little to say today but stay until mid-evening, then I delay going home by dropping into the cafeteria in the main hospital for a meal.

It is beef casserole; a few recognisable vegetables at least, rice – I am lucky to get that as they are closing the hot food section for the night. The coffee is good, strong and steamy, and I people-watch.

During the day the cafeteria feels almost cheerful, full of the noise and bustle missing from the palliative care unit. Now, there are staff on late breaks, fatigue set into lines on their faces. A woman wearing a hospital gown and headscarf is at the table opposite me, an IV pole on wheels to her side, and three people that bear a striking resemblance sit with her, laughing, but strained. An older man stares into the distance, alone like me. I recognise the purple bruises under his eyes – tiredness adds a deeper hue to mine every day. A young couple huddle together, hands wrapped around coffee beakers. She is crying, and I imagine their story: their baby in neonatal care, or one of their parents in ICU.

Visitors aren't here this late for happy reasons. Can we compare our sadness and challenges with those of others? Maybe I'm one of the lucky ones because you and I have had thirty-four years together and we've still got a little time left?

I don't feel lucky. Grief stews in my stomach and I can't finish my meal. Should I go back to your room and spend the night on the recliner?

I scratch at my knuckles, skin itchy from constant sanitising: on entering the hospice, after blowing my nose, ahead of touching the ice machine, before and after going to the toilet.

Home has little appeal, but it wins over the hospice.

I'm tired but won't sleep well fighting my worries. The past—Meaghan, Stephanie, Ebony, my breakdown—and what's ahead—your passing and all the things I will need to cope with alone.

We'd imagined two more children after Meaghan and overstretched our budget to buy this house with four bedrooms and three living areas, on its large block in a good school zone. But we couldn't fall pregnant again, then we lost Meaghan, and soon you'll be gone too.

It will take months to go through each room, the garage and garden shed, gifting some of your things to our extended family and your friends, donating others to charity. It will give me something to fill my time outside of work, but it will do little to fill the hole in my heart.

I know the house is far too large for only me, but it is where we were happiest as a couple and a family, and it holds wonderful memories. Better to pack it with rescue dogs and cats than move? Another thing to think about.

I go into your study and check your emails, then drift around the room looking at the photos and artwork you have on display. My head feels top-heavy, brain-sore, and I rest it against the wall, knocking your framed diploma. It falls face down, glass shattering on the floor. Fragments imbed my skin as I retrieve it, checking for damage beyond the glass. Turning it over, I see something taped to the backboard. An ordinary envelope, except it can't be that ordinary if it's secreted, can it?

My clumsy fingers rip it off, and open. Inside is another lined sheet with Stephanie's handwriting. Dread makes my stomach do a dive.

She had written four words: *I kept our secret.*

'What secret?'

Silence is my answer.

'Whose secret, Guy? Meaghan's? Or yours?'

My throat tightens. I claw at my chest against the feeling of it caving in, fingertips pulsing with the pounding of my heart under my skin. Struggling to breathe.

I picture you and the girls. Stephanie was at our place every day and you treated the two girls like sisters, equals for your attention. You helped them with homework, shuttled them to netball, were more patient than Ebony or me when it came to shopping for special dresses or shoes, which gave us a good laugh. You dodged their tantrums, but were always ready with the first-aid kit.

I thought Stephanie was the second daughter we never had. But this tells me she wasn't.

I think of Ebony yesterday. Her expression, words. I need to know what she meant. What she knows. And then I am back at her front door, unaware of anything in between.

'Please, Logan.'

He flinches. I have grasped his hand too tightly.

'I need to speak with her.'

He presses his lips together, then pushes the door, ushering me in. He makes coffee while Ebony and I sit at the kitchen table.

No one speaks until Logan moves to the doorway. 'I'll leave you to it.'

He gives Ebony a pointed look that I read as, *Hear her out*.

'What happened to us, Ebs?'

Her eyes well. Silence hangs for so long that I don't think she'll answer. Then she mumbles, 'You said you didn't want to see me anymore.'

Ever since Meaghan's death and my breakdown, there have been things I can't imagine or recall doing that you've had to tell me I've done, Guy. Acts of a self-centred, unreliable, flaky woman. But this is unbelievable. And I remember it differently.

I shake my head.

Ebony sighs. 'I wanted too much from you. I was leaning on you, sapping your energy, and there was nothing but the past left between us…that's the message you sent me through Guy.'

'No,' I cut her off. 'He said *you* wanted me to leave you alone. You couldn't bear having me around.'

'I'd never say that, Darcy.'

We clutch each other's hand. I think about Stephanie's notes, hidden by you, and what I suspect. I wonder if she knows more.

'I miss them both so much.' Her eyes overfill and tears streak her face.

I kept our secret. Whatever that secret was, Ebony can never find out.

We talk for hours. About our girls, about us as girls. Our focus is happy memories, until Ebony's face clouds.

'She was seeing someone, Darcy.'

My heart thuds. *Someone* implies she doesn't know who.

'An older man. Married.'

'How do you know?' Incredibly, my voice sounds normal.

A smile on her lips. 'You just do, when it's your daughter, don't you?'

I had always known when Meaghan had a new crush or was going through a breakup, such as high school relationships go. And it wasn't limited to just that part of her life – I like to think I intuited all her highs and lows.

'Yes,' I agree.

'Steph was heartbroken when Megs died. It was like part of her died then, too. The rest of her went a year later.'

Guilt probably compounded the pain of losing her best friend. I can't help considering if she could have been remorseful for something over and above sleeping with you, Guy.

I picture Meaghan sprawled lifeless on the rocks, and jolt when my mobile rings inside my handbag. Digging it out and reading an unfamiliar number, my pulse is jumpy, hands shaky – the usual Pavlov-like reaction to phone calls since your diagnosis. Is your end near? Have you slipped away?

Heat spreads through my body, flushing my face and dotting my forehead with perspiration. Not shock or fear or a menopausal flush. It is rage in anticipation that you have beaten me to the truth.

'Mrs Moordish?'

'Yes.'

'How are you tonight?' The male voice is fake-friendly, his words scripted.

'Who is this?'

His answer is convoluted, something about good things underway for Melbourne's homeless youths. He eventually makes a pitch on behalf of a charity I have donated to before, and finally I get a word in. 'It's not a good time. My husband is dying.'

He is apologising as I disconnect.

Ebony and I pick up our conversation, talk until midnight and pledge never to lose touch again. When I go home, I manage solid sleep for a change.

I skip breakfast, dress, drive and park, ordering my mind. As I walk to the hospice entrance, frost glistens on the lawn in the warm sun under an azure sky. The bright spring morning clashes with my mood.

'He had a good night,' the nurse tells me.

I nod and smile.

'He's talking this morning.' She leans in. 'They do this… have days when we can almost imagine them going home. They can hang on for weeks, months, and your husband was so fit and strong before, wasn't he?'

I do my nod-and-smile routine again, and she breezes away with her clipboard.

In your room, I am falsely cheerful. Put on your favourite CD – 'Hidden Things' by Paul Kelly and The Messengers. You squeeze my hand when I sit down. A strong, dry grip, with feeling.

'You look good.' Your voice is croaky. I feed you some ice.

We talk, or mainly I talk, inconsequential things circling into memories. Your eyes are clear and focused. Now or never.

'I'm going to tell you a story, Guy. Tell me what you think.'

A frown puckers between your eyebrows.

I soften my tone. 'There was a man who loved his wife and daughter very much. He and his wife wanted more children, but it wasn't to be, and the daughter's kindergarten friend gradually became part of the family, like another daughter.'

A pause hangs, then I add, 'Let's call her Jayne.'

I don't know if you remember Stephanie's middle name but your feet wriggle under the light blanket. Bare toes poke out. I cover them and go on.

'Jayne grew into a confident, intelligent, attractive teenager. Somehow, someday, the relationship between the man and Jayne shifted. I'd say it *became romantic*, but that glorifies statutory rape, doesn't it, Guy?'

You gesture to your mouth. I give more ice, then stand where we have direct eye contact.

'No, it's not –'

I press a finger to your cracked lips. 'Shush. It's my story.'

More foot wiggling.

'I think the man's daughter found out and the girls fought, and tragically the daughter fell to her death.'

All colour drains from your face. My words are hitting the mark. Talking abstractedly helps. It is someone else's family and heartbreak I'm describing.

'Jayne kept her secrets—the sexual liaison, the fight, the way her friend died—until she couldn't cope anymore. You could say that the man was morally responsible for the deaths of both girls. *At least*.'

Your hands are twisting mid-air.

'How's my story sound, Guy?'

We stare at each other. I sway my head.

'Oh, that's right. The man didn't know how much his young victim had told her mother, his wife's best friend, so it was imperative that they be kept apart. He particularly played on his wife's previous breakdown as he subtly, systematically manipulated her over a very long time. Made her question her own mind and become reliant on him. It mostly worked. She believed that her friend wanted nothing to do with her and, without that vital friendship, she disengaged. She performed at her job, but little more.'

'I'm –'

'You're what?' My voice is hard. '*Sorry?*'

You reach again, and I retreat. Your eyes shine with tears.

'I had a good sleep last night. First good sleep in weeks. Then in that state between solid sleep and waking, I imagined my options.'

I point out harshly, 'You are dying, so there's no point involving the police – it'd never get to court. And I won't hurt Ebony and Logan more than what your actions have already done.'

You moan.

'A few days ago, I wondered if I had the inner strength to put a pillow over your face to stop your suffering. This morning, I thought about a pillow over your face to *make* you suffer – and I could do it, too. But dawn broke and I lay there thinking some more.'

'Ice…please,' you beg.

I laugh; there'll be no more of that from me.

'I decided my best revenge is letting you know that I know what you did and what you caused.'

I give a grim smile.

'A mother knows, Guy. You let me think I was mad. You probably set up my breakdown when I was right all along: Meaghan's death wasn't a simple accident. You made your mind up to do whatever it took to stop me picking away and finding the truth.'

I slow down, emphasising, 'But now I have.'

You take a wheezing breath and heave it out.

'I hope it takes weeks for you to waste away and I hope it's excruciating.'

You do a string of juddering inhalations and exhalations.

'I can only hope that our Meaghan had no idea about your thing with Steph until the day they fought, and what she went through was quick – though it can't have been painless.'

You flinch and cry out, distressed. Good.

'It wasn't quick for Steph, Ebony, Logan or me. And that's why I'll come in each day to watch your misery.'

I wait for the air mattress to fill and lean in to whisper, 'You're dead to me.'

PREVIEW OF TELL ME WHY

If you enjoyed *Murder In The Midst*, you might also like Sandi Wallace's Georgie Harvey and John Franklin series. Here is a preview from the first instalment *Tell Me Why*.

FRIDAY 12 MARCH

CHAPTER ONE

In her dream, she was still plain and plumpish, her hair streaked with grey. Beyond that, though, everything seemed off-kilter. The first thing she noticed was that she floated above herself as she stood in a paddock. She was without her obligatory glasses and wore a floral housedress, not overalls. The images in her dream distorted and reshaped and became even more unreal. Huge sunflowers covered what would really be their well-trampled top paddock. These flowers grew so abnormally bright that they glowed like miniature suns, and she had to shield her eyes with her hand. The brightness became hot, so hot that she moved a forearm over her face.

Then the cat growled, a long, guttural note that sounded a warning. He nipped her finger and roused her from the dream. More asleep than awake, she soothed him. What had upset the amiable puss?

Her husband shook her. She sat up in bed, puzzled. As she donned her glasses, she saw that he'd pulled on work boots and a woollen jumper over his long pyjamas.

'Quick!' he yelled, shutting their bedroom window.

They reached the front verandah but couldn't see anything for the hedge around the house except an orange flush in the night sky. They could feel the intense heat and hear the sinister sound of uncontrolled flames.

From the picket fence they saw billows of smoke. Several sheds were alight. Her husband sprinted for the hose; she for the telephone, to call the local fire captain.

Panic clutched at her chest while she filled buckets of water. Her knees nearly buckled as she dashed towards the outbuildings.

Which first?

The hay shed was fully involved; a lost cause.

The barn or machinery shed?

No animals in the barn tonight.

The latter, then, as it held the combustibles and expensive equipment.

She dumped the water. It did nothing but sizzle. She ran back to the house, detoured to the water trough and returned with soaked woollen blankets. She crashed into a wall of heat; so fierce it scorched her eyes.

As the hay shed erupted, it sent embers in every direction. She protected her face from those missiles of fire with her arm, mimicking her dream persona.

Wind fanned the roaring tongues, adding to the crescendo.

She coughed as smoke filled her lungs. Fire merged the sweet odours of hay and timber with acrid fumes of fuel, pesticides and rubber. Her eyes watered.

'Where are you?' she cried out to her husband. 'Are you safe?'

She fought the flames harder. She would never give up – on him or the farm.

Above the bellow of the fire and rupturing structures and terrified shrieks of sheep and cattle, she couldn't hear a thing. Throat blistered with heat, smoke and yelling for her husband, she couldn't tell if she managed to make a sound or if the screams were only in her head.

Then, a hand clasped her shoulder and something struck her temple. She crumpled to the ground.

CHAPTER TWO

Senior Constable John Franklin had been cooped up with Paul Wells for hours. Too long without a smoke or coffee because Constable-fast-track-Wells was driving and he didn't pay much attention to those who wore fewer than three stripes on their epaulette.

But that wasn't why Franklin wanted to throttle him. It was because Wells measured time, distance, temperature, power poles and countless other things. Plus he was a rigid perfectionist with as much personality as a dead carp. Franklin's workmates rated the bloke's neurotic traits with fingernails scratching down a blackboard. His two consecutive rest days relegated to distant memories by the OCD freak, he ruled it much worse.

'Four and a half minutes,' Wells said. He tapped his watch.

Franklin groaned. So today's general patrol took five minutes longer than the previous trip – *big deal*.

'Should not have stopped for Charlie Banks…'

And that's the difference between a copper from the country and a cockhead from the big smoke.

Franklin tuned out.

A lonely bugger, poor Charlie often wanted to chew their ears. On this occasion it was about his dog's arthritis, but it was just an excuse for company. Yet Wells evidently thought the schedule more important than a quick chat with the old codger.

Franklin scrutinised the intense constable as he unclipped his seatbelt. The bloke was third-generation cop with dad, uncles and grandfather all among the brass. Odds-on he'd be promoted and back to the city before most coppers learned to scratch themselves. They wouldn't improve him, so somehow they'd have to bide time until he moved on.

Granted, the real problem today wasn't Wells. It came from him. Because he was the single parent of a hormonal teenager with attitude and because after sixteen years in the same country town, he still wore a uniform. He chatted to lonely folk, changed light globes, chopped wood and mowed lawns for elderly widows, pointed the radar for hours on end and sorted out the same drunks, the same domestics. Those were the good days. One of his blackest days had seen him as pallbearer at the funeral of a road victim who was also a mate from the footy club. All a far cry from where he'd planned to be by his mid-thirties.

Some days start badly and end up your worst nightmare. She should have seen the ladder in her new pantihose when she pulled them on this morning—hell, the need to wear a bloody skirt and heels itself—as a damn omen. A sign that she'd end up here, two beers down, stomach clenched while she cursed Narkin.

'Bastard.'

The bartender shot her a glare, not the first for that afternoon.

She hadn't meant to say it aloud and grimaced. She resumed pushing the penne pasta around her plate.

Flight of the Bumblebee pealed. She fished through her bag and frowned at the mobile screen. Number withheld. She thumbed the call switch to answer.

'Georgie Harvey.'

'It's Ruby here.'

Georgie cringed. She had avoided the older woman since yesterday but was caught now.

'Michael and I are hoping you'll look up Susan…'

What was her name? Susan Petticoat, Prenticast? Her neighbour Ruby's supposedly missing friend. Whatever; Georgie wasn't inclined to drive to Hicksville on a wild-goose chase.

She was saved by Ruby's cry of *'You silly duffer! What've you done?'*

The phone clunked. Georgie necked some beer and considered hanging up. She couldn't.

'I'll have to ring back, love.'

The call topped off a crap day. Now she felt guilty about dodging her neighbours to boot.

Disgruntled, Georgie scanned the room. It ought to have been a wood-panelled bar with punters using the pool table, old-timers arguing companionably over the footy, the call of a horse race on the radio; cheerful, noisy and as comfortable as worn slippers. Not this stark, trendy joint, with its white paint, stainless-steel counter, blond-wood seats, piped music and ultra-slick patrons. Even the barman's hair had encountered an oil spill. But this was the closest pub to the courts, and a beer was what she'd needed after her run-in with Narkin.

She speared a mouthful of pasta. It was cold and tasted like spicy cardboard. She pushed the bowl aside.

'Can't smoke in here,' the bartender said.

Georgie glanced at the unlit ciggie between her fingers. She hadn't realised she'd reached for it. She wouldn't have lit up; it was just that beer and smokes fit together perfectly. Pity smoking in pubs had been outlawed. What'd be next, inside people's homes or Melbourne's entire central business district? And was it really a health agenda or simply political?

She flicked her black lighter.

'I wouldn't.' The voice came from behind.

She grinned as Matt Gunnerson slipped onto a stool and held up two fingers with a nod and smile.

'How's crime this week, Matt?' The barman had shot daggers at Georgie since her arrival yet beamed as he greeted Matty.

'It's keeping me out of the dole queue.'

Both men laughed. The barman served two Coronas, and Matty slapped his shoulder in that matey way of his. Georgie marvelled at his easy charm, a handy attribute for an up-and-coming crime reporter. She could do with a dose if she ever cracked a real writing gig, as opposed to scripting and editing boring business resources.

They clinked bottles and swallowed in unison.

Matty commented, 'Didn't go well then, Gee?'

'Have I got *loser* plastered here?' She slashed a line across her forehead.

'Which magistrate did you get?'

'Narkin.'

'Ah.' Matty's sigh summed up fronting Pedantic Percy, as he was dubbed within the legal circle. By reputation he found against self-represented defendants – Murphy's Law, she drew him.

'Ah,' she mimicked. She tapped the file before her and said, 'Laird –'

'Laird's your ex-cop?'

'Yeah. He argued that Pascoe Vale Road's notorious for metallic reflection distorting radar readings. But their expert rebutted.'

'And Pedantic Percy agreed with theirs?' When she grimaced, he added, 'So you lost. No surprise. You *are* a lead foot.'

'I'm not that bad.'

'Sure…'

'Well, maybe I am,' she conceded. 'Anyway, I copped a fine, plus legals, though I *just* saved my licence.'

'Have you spoken to AJ yet?'

Georgie froze. Adam James Gunnerson, her live-in lover, also happened to be his brother. And he currently ranked high on her taboo list.

She was never happier to hear the *Bumblebee* tune.

While Georgie foraged for her phone, she noticed the sky had clouded over. In the tradition of Melbourne's contrary weather, the beautiful autumn day gyrated to bleak. Pedestrians on William Street scurried for shelter from the downpour or sprinted towards the train station. Except for one woman; she walked on in measured strides, stare fixed on the horizon of skyscrapers, bitumen and traffic lights. It was something Georgie would do.

'It's me again. Ruby.'

Damn. I should've known.

'Michael and I were wondering… Well, will you go to Daylesford for us?'

'I'm sorry, Ruby. Can't talk.'

'What was that about?' Matty asked after she disconnected.

'Nothing.'

Georgie squirmed. She couldn't avoid her neighbours

forever. But it was easier to avoid the conversation than turn them down flat.

Just as it was easier to run from AJ's kicked-dog eyes.

Georgie evaded Matty's inquisition by heading for the cigarette vending machine in the tiny passageway to the toilets. It was one of those days when she'd need more than her ten (or so) Benson & Hedges allowance. She fed the machine a fistful of gold coins and pushed the button.

In the ladies' room, she pulled a brush through her hair, changed her mind and messed it up. She smoothed on lip gloss and examined her reflection in the mirror. She tried a smile, then tweaked her silky black top.

Georgie leaned forward and held up thumb and index finger to make an L on her forehead. Then realised it was backwards. She couldn't even get that right.

Definite loser.

'Um, John. Got a tick?' Tim Lunny said, crooking his finger.

Franklin's stomach flipped. Was he in trouble again? Or worse: about to be permanently rostered on with Wells?

Fuck no, anything but being stuck with that wanker.

He followed Lunny into his office and dropped onto the single visitor's chair clear of paperwork, discarded uniform or fishing tackle.

The sergeant aligned and re-aligned a stack of files. Finally, he said, 'Well, you see. Oh, hell, mate. Kat's –'

'What's wrong with Kat?' Franklin straightened, alarmed.

'It's nothing like that. She's in a bit of strife –'

'Shit. What is it this time?'

'She and her two cronies took a five-finger discount at Coles.'

Franklin groaned, raking his sandy-coloured hair. The trio had received a day's suspension for smoking in the school toilets three weeks ago and he'd grounded his daughter for a month. He'd given her time off for good behaviour, and here she was, caught shoplifting days later.

'She's in Vinnie's office,' Lunny added, patting him awkwardly.

Franklin clamped his jaw, squashed on his cap and plucked keys for the marked four-wheel drive from the board.

The ninety-second drive felt protracted. And so did the walk of fucking humiliation from the truck through the car park to the innards of the supermarket. Never before had he been as conscious of the downside of living and working in such an intimate community. He knew scores of Daylesford's permanent residents after so long in town.

Tight-chested, Franklin pushed through the two-way door to the labyrinth of offices and storerooms.

He and Vinnie shook hands, then the store owner cut to the chase. 'Frankie, we don't need to take this further for a handful of Mars Bars.'

Franklin lifted his palms and let them drop.

'C'mon, the girls are pretty upset,' Vinnie coaxed, then frowned. '*Except* Narelle King. If it was her alone,' he mimed spitting, 'I'd tell you to throw the book.'

'I don't know –'

'Frankie, Frankie! Put the fear of God in them and then let it be. Go!'

Still undecided, Franklin thrust open Vinnie's door. He saw Kat flanked by her partners in crime on the sofa. While she glared, Lisa turned grey-white and Narelle reclined, blasé.

'You two.' Franklin jerked his head at Lisa and Narelle. 'Out.'

When they'd gone, he used his daughter's formal name. 'Katrina. What happened?'

She scowled harder.

He waited.

Kat clasped a hunk of her long hair. She twirled crimped blonde strands in front of her face, looking through him with clones of his own eyes. While biased and blind to their many similarities, Franklin considered her a stunner. But she was ugly with insolence now.

He faced away and leaned on Vinnie's desk. He counted to ten, then twenty. When he turned, his daughter hadn't budged.

'What am I doing wrong?'

Parents had to shoulder some blame. It ate him up to realise he'd failed her somehow.

She eye-rolled.

'Smoking, now this. What next?'

Franklin hated to see Kat make mistakes. Her next rebellious act could end in heartbreak.

She sniffed.

'I've got nothing to say to you.' The utter disappointment in his voice made her flinch.

Finally, a reaction.

Franklin pulled open the door. Narelle stumbled, caught eavesdropping.

'We're going to the station.'

The instant Kat brought Narelle King home, Franklin had identified her as a brazen troublemaker. It wasn't her bottle-blonde hair, bazooka boobs or that she carried a street-savvy sophistication from living in Melbourne until she was thirteen. Pure and simple, she'd failed Franklin's attitude test then and perpetually since. Even so, he recognised the futility of forbidding Kat's friendship with King. You don't give your teenage daughter yet another reason for defiance.

He seized the scruff of King's neck and pushed her forward. Lisa Cantrell snuffled as she trudged in the rear. Franklin sympathised with her. Studious and timid, she was an odd fit with the other two.

Franklin shepherded the girls to the truck, feeling as

miserable as Lisa. His aim was to let them imagine the worst possible outcome, while he tried not to think about local gossipmongers. He hid behind dark sunglasses and the peak of his police cap and zipped through the roundabout and two blocks to the station.

Slumped on the stool next to Matty, Georgie chomped peanuts and surveyed her companion in the mirror. His face was animated. Everyone else in this bar appeared happy too. It only made her crappy mood spiral further.

Outside was the same story. The brief shower had ceased. The road steamed warm air. After five on a Friday afternoon, the working week surrendered to the weekend. Men ripped off ties and undid top buttons. Women greeted friends as if they hadn't seen them for a month. There was saccharine sweetness all around but for her.

She slugged beer. Then the brew curdled.

Fight or flight?

Why not both?

Take time out from my messed-up life while I do a favour for Ruby. That works for me.

'I'm outta here.' Georgie slammed down her Corona, spilling it onto the stainless top.

'Need a lift, Gee?'

'Nuh, ta, I've got the Spider. Besides, you're not going anywhere near where I'm headed.'

'Where's that?'

'Daylesford.'

Before he could ask why, she hoisted handbag and court file, pecked his cheek and threaded her way to the exit.

'Gee!'

Surprised, she spun around. Half the pub froze.

'Should you be driving?' Matty pointed to the abandoned beer.

'I'll take my chances,' Georgie said, then mustered what dignity she could and merged into the commuter exodus on William Street.

We hope you enjoyed the opening of *Tell Me Why* and would like to read more. *Black Cloud* is the latest and fourth instalment in the Georgie Harvey and John Franklin series.

Dear reader,

We hope you enjoyed reading *Murder In The Midst*. Please take a moment to leave a review, even if it's a short one. Your opinion is important to us.

Discover more books by Sandi Wallace at https://www.nextchapter.pub/authors/sandi-wallace

Want to know when one of our books is free or discounted for Kindle? Join the newsletter at http://eepurl.com/bqqB3H

Best regards,

Sandi Wallace and the Next Chapter Team

More of Sandi Wallace's short crime stories are in:
On The Job

For your copy, please head to:
http://mybook.to/onthejob

ACKNOWLEDGMENTS

First, a heartfelt shout-out to you, my lovely readers. Your wonderful messages, emails and reviews keep me writing. I'd love you to join me on Facebook and Instagram or follow my website.

It wasn't until I started entering short crime stories in contests that I realised how challenging the craft is – and just how fun and addictive it can be. So I'm grateful for competitions such as Sisters in Crime Australia's Scarlet Stiletto Awards for the opportunity to hone my short story skills. Since winning my first Scarlet in 2013, I have gone on to have a series of rural crime thrillers and two volumes of short crime stories published, and I've collected more awards for my short and long-form fiction. There is no denying the inspiration to keep doing what I love that each of these honours has gifted me.

My appreciation also goes to Judy Elliot, Raylea O'Loughlin and Sharon Gurry who generously give their feedback on early drafts of my short stories and novels, and to Marianne Vincent for her keen eye over this collection. And of course, sincere thanks to the team at Next Chapter.

Always last, but never least, cheers to Glenn.

ABOUT THE AUTHOR

Sandi Wallace has been hooked on crime fiction and dreamed of being a crime writer since about the age of six, and now lives that dream. She is currently at work on a standalone psychological thriller…when ideas for a short crime story or new rural crime thriller aren't beckoning for her attention. Sandi loves life in the stunning Dandenong Ranges outside of Melbourne with her husband.

Connect with Sandi at

Website www.sandiwallace.com
Amazon www.amazon.com/author/sandiwallace
Goodreads www.goodreads.com/author/show/8431978.Sandi_Wallace
Facebook www.facebook.com/sandi.wallace.crimewriter
Instagram www.instagram.com/sandiwallacecrime
Pinterest www.pinterest.com.au/sandiwallace_crimewriter/

Lightning Source UK Ltd.
Milton Keynes UK
UKHW021900131220
375014UK00012B/887/J